SHELLY WOTA

MEMORIES AT THE MANOR

www.writeandreleasepublishing.com

DEDICATION

I would like to dedicate this book to my mom
Anne Caliguire (Peltier)

Secondly:
I would like to thank Chester and Carlo for all their input,
very much appreciated

Finally:
I would also like to thank my sister Stephanie for the two ideas
she suggested

CHAPTER 1

"I'm very pleased with how things have been going these past three years," Gina said to Arthur, during their weekly meeting which they held out in the gazebo that Arthur and Mr. Locke built two years ago. "It amazed me," she continued. "I never would have thought that only five years ago I was preparing to go to London for college." "I know what you mean," added Arthur. "If you would have asked me where I would be and what I would be doing six or seven years down the road, I probably would had looked confused and shrugged my shoulders. Coming from a broken home with very little to look forward to, I was literally thrown into this. Don't get me wrong, I love what I'm doing." "I know," replied Gina. "I never could have done it without you and my parents. I have been blessed." "That's what my grandma has often said since I started college. She and mom have been a tremendous support for me," stated Arthur. "I couldn't ask for a better business partner and friend." "I feel the same," added Gina.

"We both have our lists of what needs to be done before spring planting. I suggest we get started and when we meet up for lunch we can catch up with what can wait until you get back Friday. Be sure to tell Christine hello and don't let me forget to give you the birthday present I have for her." "Are you sure you don't mind that I will be gone for three days?" asked Arthur. "Don't give it another thought," added Gina. "Jr.

will be coming in tomorrow. You'll probably pass him on the highway. Just have a great time. See you at lunch."

Gina was so engrossed in her work; she didn't hear her father calling her for lunch. He had to literally walk up to her and tap her on her shoulder. "Oh, you startled me," exclaimed Gina. "I called you, but you didn't hear me, so I had to walk all this way to tell you that your mother has lunch ready," stated her father. "Did you call Arthur?" Gina asked. "He had already gone into the sun room, where your mother has the lunch laid out. Hurry, you know your mother won't serve until we're all there," replied her father. "Just let me wash up and I will be right in," added Gina. "Time sure flew by fast. It seems like I just got out here, Gina mumbled to herself as she washed up."

"This looks like a delicious lunch; cucumber sandwiches, fruit and your special cupcakes," announced Gina, as she took a seat. "I didn't realize I was so hungry." "Dig in everyone," Mrs. Locke said. "There's more if you need it." "I will definitely be going for seconds," stated Arthur. "I have some physically demanding work to do this afternoon, and I will need all the strength I can get." "Me, too," added Mr. Locke. "I will be helping Arthur this afternoon." "I will be sure to bring out cool drinks a little later," mentioned Mrs. Locke. "Gina, what are your plans for this afternoon?" "Well, after I finish what I was working on this morning, I want to go up to my studio and do some painting, if I am not needed elsewhere," added Gina. "No problem, we've got it all covered," put in her mother. "I will also bring you up a cool drink later." "Thanks, mom," Gina replied.

Around dinnertime Gina had finally decided on how she was to present her thoughts of what she wanted to put to canvas. It was the transition of what has happened over the past 5 years. Now that she has a plan of action, she felt confident as to how she will start the actual painting. She's in no hurry to finish it, but cannot wait to see how it progresses. Leaving it for the three days that Arthur will be away and while Jr. is visiting can give her a clear head on how to start. She's excited, but does not want anyone to know, so she has to keep that fact from her mother.

The next morning, after a light breakfast of toast, fruit, cereal, orange juice and coffee, Arthur set off for London. Gina finished a few tasks and decided to check on the preparations for Jr.'s visit. Her mom and Trisha put the finishing touches on the guest room that he occupies whenever he visits. Meanwhile Gina reviewed her itinerary for what needed to be done while Arthur was away. She knows Jr. will be only too happy to help. She loves the times when they work together. She dreams of when he will be living there permanently. During this visit, she and Jr. will need to find a quiet spot in order to continue discussing their engagement and when they want to get married. They told each other that they want to marry at the manor, since it has been the basis of their relationship. They don't want anyone to know their plans until all has been arranged so as not to spoil the surprise.

CHAPTER

2

Arthur arrived in London on Wednesday about noon. He was in time to have lunch with his mother and grandmother. Christine lives with his mother and grandmother, but she was still at work. Arthur decided to pick her up and take her out for a quiet romantic dinner in a restaurant he recently heard great reviews about. His mother had planned a surprise dinner for Christine's birthday for the next evening. Arthur cannot believe how blessed he is in his relationship with Christine. When she had to go back to Scotland to help while her mother was ill, Arthur actually considered moving there and securing a job for as long as Christine would be there. Sadly, her mother passed away after a year. Christine felt guilty about leaving her family, but her father insisted that one of her mother's last wishes would be that she would return to London to continue with her career plans.

During dinner, Arthur brought Christine up to date on all that he and Gina have accomplished since her last visit to the manor. Afterwards they went for a walk in a nearby park which was close to his grandmother's. They wanted to discuss their plans for announcing their engagement and that they also want to have the engagement party at the manor. However, they didn't know that Gina and Jr. were also planning to announce their engagement and they also planned to have their engagement party at the manor.

4

Christine mentioned to Arthur that her father and brothers are planning a visit to London in about three weeks when Scotland has a bank holiday. "Do you think they could stay for a weekend at the manor?" she asked Arthur. "I have been telling dad all about what you and Gina have been doing and it would be good if he could actually see it. And my brothers, they have never stayed at an authentic manor house and are so excited. Would you talk to Gina and her parents when you get back? I need to tell dad so he can make their final plans." "I don't think it would be a problem at all," Arthur stated. "I know Mr. & Mrs. Locke would love to have some youngsters around. I'll call them when we get back from our walk." "That sounds perfect," added Christine.

"Since I will be here for a few more days, I will spend the days with mom and grandma, and then we can have the evenings to ourselves. Is there anything you would like to do?" Arthur asked her. "I noticed that there is a new garden market open which sells crafts as well as food stuffs. We can go after work one day and maybe you can pick up anything you will need for the dinner you want to make for your mom and grandma. On another evening maybe we can go for a short boat ride down the Thames," suggested Christine. "I think that could be arranged," stated Arthur. "Mom is planning to make my favorite fried chicken with mashed potatoes and garden peas." "Maybe we can pick up some peas at the garden market," suggested Christine.

For the rest of his days off, Arthur and Christine spent as much time together as they could. The last night of his visit, Arthur and Christine made dinner, since both his mom and grandma had been very busy and Arthur felt they could use a break. He couldn't help noticing that his grandma was getting slower in her advanced age and that walking was becoming more difficult. Sometimes during the day she could be found sitting in her favorite chair. He brought up his concerns with his mother and she told him it was just age catching up with his grandmother. Otherwise she was in good health.

After the delicious dinner Arthur and Christine made, they went for a long walk. She surprised Arthur and told him that she had the weekend off and suggested that she leave with him the next day and get a ride back to London with Jr. Sunday evening.

CHAPTER 3

The day Arthur left, Mrs. Locke and Trisha headed out to the garden shed to make sure they had all the available tools they would need for the pre-spring clean-up before planting. Mrs. Locke enjoyed working with Trisha. She told Mr. Locke that she almost thought of Trisha as a daughter. She found Trisha to be a very hard worker. Earlier in the year Trisha had mentioned to Mrs. Locke that she had decided to go to Croydon College into the Hospitality and Tourism course. Mrs. Locke credited Dorothy for raising such a diligent and serious person. With her attention to detail and strong work ethic, Mrs. Locke felt that Trisha would do very well in her chosen career path. She would definitely be missed when she moves to London to attend college. Mrs. Locke and Gina both gave Trisha an open invitation to visit anytime. And, she could bring her mother and brothers along as well.

Mr. Locke went over the list that Arthur left of the things that needed to be done. In addition to sharpening the gardening tools that Mrs. Locke brought out, he was also to make sure all the supplies needed were available. Mrs. Locke and Trisha also made a list of any other supplies they may need. They decided to all go to Luton to make the purchases. As a treat, when she and Trisha have finished their shopping, they would go for tea and cakes while Mr. Locke went to the gardening shop. He would meet up with the ladies when he had finished. They promised to save him some cake.

"Did you manage to get everything on the list?" Mrs. Locke asked her husband. "I sure did, plus a few more things," answered Mr. Locke. "Well, sit down and enjoy tea with us," added Mrs. Locke. "These desserts are scrumptious," mentioned Trisha. "I can definitely put away one or two," stated Mr. Locke. "Who knew shopping was such hungry work."

"Are you excited about going to college and living in London?" asked Mrs. Locke. "Oh, yes, for sure," answered Trisha. "And a little nervous, but Gina has been telling me things about Croydon College that she feels I should know. She assures me that I will make friends quite easily. It will be different living in London, but not with my brothers. Just recently they moved in with our father and mom is now renting a small bed-sit. She did manage to secure a part-time job. It should not interfere with her visits to Calais to visit her pen pal. They seem to get along quite well." "Why do you say that?" asked Mrs. Locke. "Because mom is always in such a happy, joyful mood when she gets home from one of her visits. I tease her that maybe she has a boyfriend there," stated Trisha. "I hate to interrupt this cozy tea-time ladies, but I think we should head home," Mr. Locke said. "Yes, you are right, my dear," added Mrs. Locke as they prepared to leave the café. "It is getting late; and Trisha has to catch her bus to London for her weekend with her mom." "Mom and I planned to tour around the college, just to get the lay of the land," Trisha mentioned to the Lockes.

CHAPTER

4

After Mr. & Mrs. Locke left with Trisha, Gina sat in the conservatory soaking up the sun, sipping her tea while contemplating her next task. She then decided that she would take Buddy for a long walk before it got too hot. Gina thought it was a good idea that they have a dog; but since Buddy was a rescue dog of undetermined age, the veterinarian figured Buddy could be about 12 years old. The whole family had noticed that at times Buddy would stop when playing to rest. Even with his favorite game of fetch, it would tire him quickly. Gina will talk to the family after Arthur gets back and suggest they get another dog.

Gina turned to Buddy and asked him if he wanted a friend. He looked at her like, what are you saying. Gina told Buddy that she thinks they will get him a friend, because sometimes they get so busy that they almost forget to take him for his walk or find time to play with him; so if he had a friend, then they can play together. "What do you think?" she asked again. Buddy barked and wagged his tail. Gina took that as a yes. "Now, Buddy, I must get to work soon, but first we will go for a walk," added Gina. "I don't want the others coming home and seeing me still sitting here." Buddy barked twice and then started walking off, making Gina catch up. Afterwards Gina went up to her studio hoping to get a couple of hours of work done. Her mom mentioned they probably wouldn't be back until just before dinner, so Gina decided that she would have dinner ready for when they got back.

Gina was so engrossed in her work that she didn't realize that the phone was ringing. Too late, she thought. If it was important the caller will either call back or leave a message. The interruption did break her concentration and when she looked at her watch, she realized it was time to start preparing dinner. She went downstairs, checked on Buddy (who was snoozing in his favorite spot), then she enclosed herself in the kitchen and prepared to wow everyone with her culinary expertise.

Everyone came home famished, and was welcomed with a most pleasant aroma coming from the kitchen. They were surprised with a chicken casserole, green salad and fresh rolls. Mrs. Locke was able to identify the spices Gina used. She praised Gina for the lovely dinner she had prepared for them. Mr. Locke complimented Gina by having seconds. Even Trisha complimented Gina by asking her for the recipe. All in all everyone agreed that it was a dinner not to be forgotten anytime soon. During dessert Gina brought up the subject of a friend for Buddy. It was decided that they would bring up the subject when Arthur came home. Gina will also get Jr.'s opinion when he arrives at the manor.

Mrs. Locke asked Gina "Wasn't Jr. supposed to be here by dinner time?" "Yes, he was," answered Gina. "He was delayed but should be here shortly. I told him I would save him some dinner, if dad hasn't eaten it all." "Don't worry, dear, I am so stuffed, Buddy will have to take me for a walk," replied her dad. "There he goes now; I don't think Buddy's barking for his walk, I think he's announcing the arrival of Jr.." "You're right there, Mr. Locke Jr. said as he walked into the kitchen. But I do think Buddy is waiting for his walk." "Gina, take Jr. out to the conservatory to enjoy the delicious dinner you made, while Trisha and I clean up. No, no, no arguments," insisted Mrs. Locke. "You cooked so we will be happy to clean up. Now out," Mrs. Locke said as she shoed Gina and Jr. out.

Gina and Jr. headed out to the conservatory. While Jr. was enjoying his dinner, Gina filled him in on what's been happening. He also agreed that Buddy was slowing down and that they should get another dog; not only as a companion for Buddy, but when Buddy is too old to be a guard dog, the new dog can take over, and then Buddy can enjoy retirement.

"Let's go for a walk before we all meet for coffee later," suggested Gina. "I'm with you there," announced Jr. while patting his stomach. "That was a very delicious dinner, my dear, and did I hear correctly, that you made it?" "Yes, I did," stated Gina. "Did you not realize that you are engaged to a woman of many talents?" "I can't wait to find out what other hidden talents you have. I will be the luckiest husband around," added Jr. "Flattery will get you everywhere," called Gina as she wandered ahead of Jr.. "Come on Jr. you're getting as slow as Buddy."

"When do you think we can tell the others of our engagement?" Jr. asked Gina. "I have the ring, so if you will consent to become my wife, we can tell them this weekend," stated Jr. as he got down on one knee. "Oh Jr.," gushed Gina. "You brought the ring. This is such a surprise. I know we want to get engaged, but; oh, this is so beautiful," said a tearful Gina as Jr. slipped the ring onto her finger. "Well, what do you think?" asked Jr. "Can we tell everyone this weekend?" "It will have to be on Saturday, because Arthur gets back Friday evening and you have to leave Sunday evening, so that just leaves Saturday. What do you think?" replied Gina. "I think Saturday would be perfect," answered Jr. while giving Gina a kiss. They lingered over their goodnight kiss, enjoying each other's company.

CHAPTER

5

Arthur was happy to hear that Christine had a three day weekend. When they got back from their walk, Christine told Arthur's mother and grandmother that she would be going to Cockernhoe with Arthur and planned to be back home Sunday evening.

Even though Arthur wanted to get an early start, his grandmother was up and made them a hearty breakfast which included pancakes, eggs, hash browns and juice and coffee or tea. After breakfast, there were hugs all around, goodbyes and wishes for a safe journey were said, with the promise to call when they arrived at the manor.

"Do you think Gina and her parents would mind that we would like to have our engagement party at the manor?" Christine asked Arthur. "No, I don't see any problem," stated Arthur. "I know Mrs. Locke would love to host a party and Trisha would be there to help with the cooking and cleaning. Trisha has become almost like family. Have I told you that she will be going to Croydon College for the Hospitality and Tourism course?" "No, you didn't," answered Christine. "That's wonderful. Don't her mother and brothers live in London?" "Yes, they do, but her brothers now live with their father; so Trisha would save on paying for accommodations since she will be staying at mom's and grandma's," replied Arthur.

"Have you thought of the day for the wedding?" Arthur asked. "I think we should have it in August. That is about eight months from now, and it would give my family time to save," answered Christine. "Since they already made plans to come for a short visit in a few weeks, eight months should be enough time to plan," "I think August does sound good," stated Arthur. "I hope we can make that decision this weekend," stated Christine. "We can have the ceremony in London, and then drive to the manor for the reception. What do you think?" asked Arthur. "Wow, I would love that, but again, do you think Mr. & Mrs. Locke would mind?" replied Christine. "I know for sure that Gina would love it, it might give her and Jr. a hint. Then we could have a double wedding. What do you think of that?" asked Arthur. "I can't wait to talk to Gina and Jr. about it," stated Christine.

Arthur and Christine arrived at the manor just as the Lockes, Trisha, Gina and Jr. were having lunch. "You arrived just at the right time, we now have two extra persons for the afternoon chores," Mr. Locke said teasingly. "You can count on us," answered Arthur. "We worked very hard this morning," added Gina. "Didn't I tell you, someone would say that?" said Arthur, turning to Christine. "It's nice to see you," added Christine, as she acknowledged everyone with a smile. "Fortunately she has a three day weekend," added Arthur. "Sit down," motioned Mrs. Locke, to the two empty chairs. "How are your grandmother and mother?" she asked. "They are well, but I've noticed that grandma is slowing down," stated Arthur. "That happens when a person ages," added Mr. Locke. "You will one day yourself, Arthur. Give them our best wishes when you get back home, please Christine."

"What were you working on?" Arthur asked Mr.Locke. "Just let me change and I'll come and help you." "That would definitely make the work get done faster with you and Jr. helping," pointed out Mr. Locke. Christine turns to Gina and offers her services. After Christine changed, she and Gina went out to the garden. Mrs. Locke and Trisha cleared the dishes then continued with the rest of the minor household chores of dusting and spot cleaning.

After a hard day's work by everyone, they sat down to a delicious pasta dinner. When coffee and dessert were served, Arthur announced that he and Christine had something they wanted to talk to everyone about.

CHAPTER

6

After Philip read the letter from his mother, he and Charlotte proceeded to make travel plans. Firstly, Charlotte said that they would leave Annabelle with Charlotte's mother, since she felt that Annabelle was too young for travelling. Charlotte told her mother that she was looking forward to the visit to London, and that she wanted to be there as support for Philip. She had researched London after she met Philip and enjoyed listening to him tell her of some of the counties where there would be some very old churches, houses and even some castle ruins. The twins were also interested and did some research of their own after they were told that Arthur (Philip's son) lives in a manor house.

Their flight to London went without any hiccups, and after collecting their luggage and clearing customs, Philip hailed one of the old style taxis to take them to his mother's home. Tired as they were, they were trying to take in as much as they could during the long drive from the airport. Philip told them they would have plenty of time to look around after they got settled. The reunion with his mother was tearful, with hugs all around. Philip had not been home since he left all those years ago. His mother welcomed Charlotte and the twins with open arms. Ushering them in, she told them that she had tea ready. Adam, the mouthpiece of the two, said that he and Aaron didn't drink tea. Philip laughed and told them that in England when they mentioned tea, it was what

Canadians would call dinner. "Great, because I'm starving," announced Adam. "First, Philip will take you to your room, you can drop off your luggage and wash up," said grandma. "Philip, you and Charlotte can have your old room and the boys can share the spare room. I hope they will be comfortable." "They'll manage," stated Philip. "Won't you, boys?" "Yea, sure," replied Adam and Aaron at the same time.

After tea, while the twins went for a walk to the nearest park, they had jet lag and couldn't settle down. Philip told them not to get lost and not to be gone too long. He, Charlotte and his mom settled in the reception room with coffee. His mom told them about her health concern and the surgery she will have to have. Her stay in the hospital will be about one week, depending on her recovery. Then she would need to go every few days for therapy. They would have about 10 days before she goes into the hospital, so Philip would have time to show his family around London. After the twins become familiar with their surroundings, they would be able to wander about on their own. Philip mentioned that one day he wanted to rent a car to take them on a day trip to Cockernhoe where he grew up. He planned to drive by the manor to give them a peek at the place he worked at when he was younger. First of all, they needed a good night's sleep. Even though the twins insisted that they were not tired, it didn't take very long before they had fallen asleep.

The next day his mother had the pre-surgery appointment. Her doctor thought it would be a good idea that Philip and Charlotte attend, since they would be looking after her after the surgery. Her doctor's office was near Camden Road market place, so they left the twins there and agreed to meet back at the huge clock in the centre of the plaza in about an hour and a half. Adam and Aaron wandered around for a bit feeling a bit lost, but Aaron considered himself to have a good memory so they were able to enjoy some of the marketplace before having to meet their parents. Adam pointed out the big bridge, which Philip said was the famous London Bridge. They were close enough to be able to cross over it. Halfway over, Charlotte stopped to look down on the Thames. She commented on how dirty it looked. Philip replied that people would dump just about anything into the river. Now there are laws that forbid any dumping plus the fines are steep.

CHAPTER 7

Before his mother was to be admitted to the hospital, Philip wanted to take his family on a short road trip. He had arranged to rent a vehicle and drive to Rumforton and Cockernhoe as well as taking a short drive past the manor. In Cockernhoe he wanted to show them the house he was born in and the local fun spots he and his friends frequented. In Rumforton he showed them the school he graduated from grade twelve. Philip reminded his family that these villages are very small, and usually why many people moved to a bigger city after graduation was to secure further education or employment. Philip said he was lucky to get a job at the manor. The villages were beautiful places to live but the job markets were very limited. After they had lunch in Luton, Philip thought it would be a treat if they were to take the ferry over to Calais, France.

Charlotte thought the villages were cute, while the twins looked bored. The drive past the manor brought them to attention. "Did you really work here?" Adam asked. "Wow, it's huge," stated Aaron. "Yes, there is a big difference in the size of houses in Cockernhoe compared to the manor," stated Philip. "In my grandfather's time, the manor employed quite a few villagers, but times have changed. The owners in my father's time only wanted the manor as a family home, not a working home." "What do you mean working home?" Charlotte asked. "It meant the family had a big garden as well as livestock, in which they would share their extra bounty with the villagers who were in need. So, not only did they hire villagers they also took care of them," explained Philip.

Dorothy surprised Trisha when she got to London by saying that they would be going over to Calais in France for the day. It had so happened that they were on the same ferry as Philip and his family. They did not know each other since Philip was at least 10 years older than Dorothy. Trisha heard the twins talking but didn't recognize the accent, so she asked them where they were from. They said they were from Canada, but their father was British and as a matter of fact he was from Cockernhoe. When Dorothy heard this she asked what their father's name was. They told her it was Philip Trowbridge. What a coincidence, Dorothy thought, of all the people she might meet on the ferry, she met one who was born in Cockernhoe. She remembered she had heard stories about the Trowbridges and the manor. So, their father must be Arthur's biological father. I must meet him, she thought. Wait until I tell Helen, that she had run into Philip Trowbridge and his family on a visit from Canada.

About that time, Philip and Charlotte were looking for the twins because they would be docking soon and Charlotte did not want to be separated from the boys. Dorothy was focused on the man and his wife, while the twins were focused on Trisha. While introductions were being made, Adam could not take his eyes off Trisha. Aaron had to nudge him to pay attention. Dorothy voiced her surprise that is such a coincidence to meet someone from the same village she was from. "It's a small world," mentioned Dorothy, "to meet someone from my small village. Who would have thought?" Philip was leery because he didn't know how much Dorothy might know of his life there and he certainly didn't want Charlotte to find out more of his past from strangers. An announcement interrupted them saying that passengers with cars should please return to them for disembarking. Adam had wanted to ask Trisha for her phone number, since they would be in England for a while. He wanted to get to know her. He asked Philip if there was a way he could find out Trisha's number. Philip believed he could ask his mother who could then call Dorothy's mother since they knew each other from Cockernhoe. Dorothy wished them a wonderful visit to England, and then she and Trisha went to where walk-ons would disembark to catch their transportation from the ferry terminal.

"Mom, did you know the Trowbridges?" Trisha asked. "No, but grandma would remember. I'll ask her when we get home," added her mother. "The twins were cute, don't you think?" stated Trisha. "Yes, they were," answered her mom. "Do you think all Canadian boys are that cute?" questioned Trisha. "It's hard to say, we do have cute boys in England, you know," replied her mom. "I know, I know," mumbled Trisha as they prepared to disembark.

Adam couldn't take his eyes off Trisha because she was very pretty and he wanted to see more of her and hopefully to get to know her better. He was beginning to devise a plan so he could see more of her. He would wait until Philip asked his mother about the people they met. It's a good thing they planned on staying in London until the end of summer.

CHAPTER

8

During dinner Mrs. Locke noticed the looks on each of the young adult's faces. They were smiling slyly to each other; Gina to Jr. and Arthur to Christine. Something's brewing here thought Mrs. Locke. As if reading her mind, Gina said she and Jr. have something they wanted to tell everyone once they got settled in the conservatory for coffee and dessert. Her mother couldn't help smiling. She was sure they were going to announce their engagement. As for Arthur and Christine, it looked like they had the same secret to share. Won't that be wonderful, Mrs. Locke thinks to herself? We can throw them a joint engagement party here at the manor.

Once everyone was seated in the conservatory, Gina announced that she and Jr. are engaged and hoped to have their engagement family dinner at the manor. Congratulations were given all around. Mr. Locke practically shook Jr.'s hand off, while Mrs. Locke hugged Gina within an inch of her life. Arthur gave Jr. a friendly slap on the back while Christine hugged Gina almost as hard as Mrs. Locke did. When Mrs. Locke noticed a questioning look pass between Christine and Arthur, she asked, "Do you and Christine have something to say?" "Well, as a matter of fact," stated Arthur, "Christine and I are also engaged and were also hoping to have the engagement dinner here." "What a surprise, who would have thought," announced Mr. Locke. "This is a happy occasion,

I think we need something stronger, to drink a toast; what do you think mother?"

Mrs. Locke was already planning the dual engagement dinner in her mind. She asked the brides-to-be what day they were thinking for their engagement dinner. Better yet, when did they plan to get married? "We hadn't really set an actual date," Gina told her mom, "but we were thinking August." "Wow," said Christine, "We were planning our wedding for August also, so as to give my dad and brothers enough notice so they can arrange time off work." "Also," added Christine, "My dad and brothers will be coming to London in a few weeks, so I was hoping they would be able to spend a few nights here at the manor." "Maybe that would be a great time to have the engagement dinner," mentioned Mrs. Locke. "What do you think?" asked Arthur as he turned to Mr. & Mrs. Locke. "Can Christine's family stay at the manor and would there be enough time to plan the dinner? Would it be too much work for you?" asked Arthur. "I say that plan suits me fine," added Jr. "What do you think, my dear?" he asked Gina. "It all sounds just splendid to me," she replied. "I guess we need to start planning. How about tomorrow, mom? Can you, Christine and I get together and start thinking of the menu?" "Since Christine is here for the weekend it would be the perfect time." "You four have made me and Mr. Locke very happy," gushed Mrs. Locke, desperately trying to hold back her emotions.

CHAPTER

9

When Trisha and her mom got back to London, Trisha was anxious to hear more about Philip and his family. She nudged her mother into asking her grandmother about the British man, who was born in Cockernhoe, and whom they met on the ferry to Calais. Dorothy was teasing Trisha that she wasn't interested in the British man as much as she was interested in one of his sons. "I admit it, mom," stated Trisha, "I did find Adam quite cute. I'll make tea while you ask grandma if she knew the Trowbridges." "All right, all right," replied her mother. "And don't forget the biscuits." "What's this about the Trowbridges?" Dorothy's mother asked. "We met a family on the ferry to Calais who were visiting from Canada and it turns out that the father was born in Cockernhoe. He had two very cute twins. His last name is Trowbridge. Did you know them or do you know anything about them?" asked Dorothy. "Yes, I do," answered her mother, "but it isn't anything I would want Trisha to know, so before she comes back, I will tell you the gist of it and then I'll sugarcoat it for Trisha. I don't see why she would need to know anything that is too personal, since she may never meet up with them again. They are probably just here for a holiday and would be leaving after a while." "Didn't you say that his mother lives in London?" asked Dorothy. "Maybe you can find out how long they will be staying." "Yes, I can do that. I'll call her tomorrow, after Trisha has gone back to

20

the manor." "Sounds good to me," replied Dorothy. "Ah, here comes the tea. I'm parched. Thanks dear," she said to Trisha. "Your mother told me that you met up with a Canadian family on the ferry, and that the father was born in Cockernhoe," Trisha's grandmother said to her. "Yes, I did know the Trowbridges. I was quite friendly with Mrs. Trowbridge, who would be the mother of Philip. Her husband worked at the manor house for a few years, and then one day he suddenly left, with no explanation to his wife. Philip was just a wee boy then, but his mother did eventually re-marry. Then when Philip was eighteen, his step-father passed away unexpectantly; so since Philip had just finished school, his mother decided to move to London, to live with her mother, but Philip had secured a job at the manor and opted to stay in Cockernhoe. He started dating Maggie Wilson, one of the kitchen maids up at the manor. Maggie was hoping that if they got married, that she would be able to quit her job as kitchen maid. She was afraid of Mr. Beavington's moods when he had been drinking. Apparently, one of the downstairs maids left without saying good bye, and Maggie overheard Mr. and Mrs. Locke discussing it late one night in the kitchen. It was suggested that Maggie take over some of the duties until a replacement could be found. She was so nervous when she had to be in the same room as Mr. Beavington, but one of her duties was to prepare the fire for the next morning's lighting. One night Mr. Beavington blocked Maggie from leaving his study. Maggie didn't know what to do, but thankfully Mr. Locke came by giving her a chance to escape. She couldn't confide in Philip; not knowing what he would do and she didn't want him to lose his job, so she did her best to stay out of Mr. Beavington's way. She succeeded for a while, but late one night, Mr. Beavington called on her to prepare the fire earlier. He knew most of the staff was celebrating Mrs. Locke's birthday in the kitchen so he felt he wouldn't be interrupted. After Maggie finished preparing the fire, she tried to leave but Mr. Beavington had locked the study door, trapping her. She begged to be able to pass saying that Mrs. Locke told her to hurry back to the celebrations. Mr. Beavington was beyond reasoning. He had been drinking all afternoon. Maggie was quietly praying that someone would come looking for her. Mr. Beavington caught her by her hair and threatened her not to tell anyone, Mr. Beavington would say that she approached him. Mrs. Beavington would believe him since it is well known that she and Philip were close. She tried telling him that she was a virgin, but he was too far gone to listen to reason. After he had his way with her he told her she better keep her mouth shut or else.

The next month Maggie believed she was pregnant, but couldn't confide in anyone. She hoped that she was just mistaken. After another month, Maggie knew for a fact that she was pregnant. Since Philip had been wanting them to become intimate, she finally gave in. Her idea was to tell Philip that he was the father of her child. When she told him, he agreed to marry her, but didn't really want to. He started drinking heavily; which affected their marriage and his job. Mr. Beavington terminated his employment. Maggie was able to work until close to the baby's arrival. After their son was born, Philip was offered a job in London. Maggie wanted to stay in Cockernhoe, so Philip left with the promise he would send for them once he got settled. When Arthur was 3 months old, Maggie received a letter from Philip asking for a divorce. Maggie did not contest it. Shortly after that she heard that he was offered a job overseas and left for Canada.

Before long Maggie met and married Malcolm Graves. Malcolm adopted Arthur. But, after all that went on at the manor and the following gossip, Malcolm and Maggie packed up and moved to London. A year later Malcolm was hit by a trolley and succumbed to his injuries, leaving Maggie a single mother."

CHAPTER

10

When Philip and his family got back to his mother's place, they were all exhausted. During dinner the twins told their grandmother about the trip with so much excitement. Neither of them had ever been on a boat, let alone a ferry boat. "Who would think that a person could travel from one country to another in so short a time and in such a totally different way?" announced Adam. "It was like black and white. Here in London I found it crowded, noisy, and rushed, but interesting. Then again, in Calais, it was like stepping back a hundred years, to a more laid back lifestyle. I know a lot has to do with the fact that London is a much bigger city and the architecture here is old and so full of history, but the architecture in Calais seemed older, and was also screaming history and with most everyone speaking French, it was a bit overwhelming at first, but after a while I got the feel of it, and felt like I belonged." "There are many buildings in London that are old and look it," pointed out his grandmother. "You just haven't seen them yet. What did you think about Calais, Aaron?" "I found it very interesting. I only wish we had more time there," stated Aaron. "I think we could find some time to go back there before returning to Canada," stated Philip. "Your mom and I didn't think either of you would like it at all, but we are pleased that you want to return."

Turning to his mother, Philip said, "You wouldn't believe who we met on the ferry; Dorothy and her daughter Trisha. They told us they lived in Cockernhoe, but now call London their home. She was a few years younger than me, but I remember that she married quite young and had Trisha and two boys." "Yes, I remember," stated his mother. "Her husband left her and went to work in Ireland. He did send money to Dorothy for child support. Dorothy worked part-time in Rumforton. After only two years her husband came back and asked for a divorce. He quickly remarried after that. When her mother took ill, Dorothy moved to London. Her ex-husband took custody of their boys. Did she recognize you?"

"I don't believe so," stated Philip. "But I would like to rent a car and drive back to Cockernhoe and Rumforton and spend a full day there showing Charlotte and the boys more of the areas where I grew up and maybe to see a little more of the manor house. We could stop at an original tea house. You did say that the Lockes still lived at the manor; do you think they would mind us stopping by and maybe getting quick tour?" "I'll call there after tea," announced his mother. "I don't think the Lockes would mind showing some Canadians around, especially since one of you is a local. It would be good for the boys to see how things were so many years ago. And, I am sure Mrs. Locke would love to show Charlotte around a typical British manor kitchen and gardens, as well as explain how things were done when she was just a young maiden, helping at the manor." "Thanks mom," replied Philip. "Please let me know if they are agreeable, then I can book a rental car."

CHAPTER

11

"Hello, Margaret, it's Sharon calling from London. How are you? Sorry it's been so long since we last chatted, but Philip and his family are here from Canada and will be staying with me for a while after my surgery. Yes, it's only minor, but I would need some help afterwards, so Philip and his family decided to come over to help. Meanwhile, Philip is going to rent a car to show his family Cockernhoe and Rumforton. He asked if I could ask you and Mr. Locke if they could stop at the manor and maybe get a quick tour," stated Sharon. "Does he know that Arthur is one of the heirs?" asked Margaret. "No, he doesn't, I wasn't sure whether I should tell him," answered Sharon. "I don't know how he would feel." "I'll speak to the rest of the family and call back as soon as I can," stated Margaret. "Thank you, that's all I could ask," replied Sharon.

While having dessert and tea out on the terrace, Mrs. Locke brought up the phone call. After telling everyone who had called, she turned to Arthur and asked what he thought of Philip and his family coming for a quick tour. At first, Arthur didn't know what to say, but promised to think about it and let Mrs. Locke know tomorrow. That's all Sharon asked. "Take your time, Philip and his family will be staying in London for a while yet," mentioned Mrs. Locke, "Also that Sharon said she will be having minor surgery and that's why Philip and his family came to London."

25

Arthur excused himself, whistled for Buddy and went out for a walk. Mrs. Locke asked Mr. Locke if he should go with him. "No, my dear," answered Mr. Locke. "I think Arthur needs this time to himself. He has a big decision to make. He was quite young when his father left, so who knows what's going on in his mind." "I think you're right," Mrs. Locke added. "He may want to call his mother and grandmother for their opinions. I'm sure he will make the right decision." She turned to Gina, "What do you think, Gina?" "Since Arthur was so young when his father left, Arthur may not have much of a memory. It would be a good idea that he calls his mom and grandmother," stated Gina.

After his walk with Buddy, Arthur went into the study to call his mother. "Hello, mom, I hope I haven't called at a bad time," stated Arthur. "No, my dear," she replied. "I was just sitting down with a cuppa. Are you calling about the fact that Philip and his family would like a tour of the manor house?" "Yes, I am," replied Arthur. "If you would rather not see him, then maybe you can arrange to be away when they arrive at the manor," answered his mother. "I think that would be a great idea," said Arthur. "I will go let Mrs. Locke know so she can call Sharon to let them know that they can stop by. Thanks mom," added Arthur. "You're the best." Arthur went into the kitchen to let Mrs. Locke know that she can call Sharon.

"Oh, hello Arthur,' stated Mrs. Locke. "Did you and Buddy have a good walk?" "We sure did, I think Buddy was getting tired out," replied Arthur. "I came to tell you that I spoke to mom and decided that you can call Sharon and let her know that Philip and his family would be welcome to stop by for a quick tour." "That's great," answered Mrs. Locke. "I will call her first thing in the morning. Is there anything you need before I retire?" "No, I'm fine, thanks Mrs. Locke," mentioned Arthur as he grabbed a muffin on his way out of the kitchen." Good night."

12

After cleaning up the breakfast dishes, Mrs. Locke phoned Sharon. "How are you this fine morning, Sharon?" she asked. "I'm just fine, thanks, and you?" replied Sharon. "I just sent Philip and his family off on another sightseeing trip. They want to see as much as they can in the time they have." "Well, I spoke to the others and they all agree that Philip and his family are welcome to come for a quick tour," mentioned Mrs. Locke. "Be sure to give us a couple of days' notice so Mr. Locke and I will be home to receive them. Anyway, Arthur and Gina plan on being away from the manor on the day of their visit." "I think that's a good idea," stated Sharon. "I will let Philip know at tea tonight, and get back to you about the day he wants to visit. Thanks so much." "No problem," replied Margaret. "We'll talk soon."

Mrs. Locke brought the family up to date about the visit Philip wants to make. "Sharon will give us a few days' notice as to when the actual day will be, so we can make arrangements," stated Mrs. Locke. "She also told me that Philip doesn't know anything about who owns the manor, and we both thought there was no reason to tell him. What do all of you think?" "Personally, I think that is for the best," added Mr. Locke. "What do you think, Gina?" "I also see no reason to tell him, since he lives in Canada now, I don't see what difference it would make. What do you think Arthur?" "I agree with all of you, there is no need for him to know."

"Good, we'll leave it as it is," put in Mr. Locke. "But, who do we say is the owner, if Philip asks? Do you think it would be terribly wrong to say that the solicitor's firm owns it?" Mrs. Locke asked. "I'll ask Jr. for advice," answered Mr. Locke. "Are we all in agreement?" Everyone nodded assent. "Great," replied Mr. Locke. "I will get back to you after I've spoken to Jr."

Just before dinner that evening, Mr. Locke mentioned that he talked to Jr. who agreed that we can say that his firm owns the manor. "I think that's a great idea," stated Mrs. Locke. "I'm kind of anxious to see how Philip is. We knew him when he was just a lad." "I heard that he married a woman in Canada and they had twins boys and much later a daughter, whom Sharon said was left in Canada with her grandmother, since she was too young to travel."

CHAPTER

13

Sharon called Margaret Saturday evening to inform her of the day Philip and his family would like to visit the manor. "Philip had booked a rental for Wednesday July 8," Sharon informed Margaret. "Would there be enough time for Arthur and Gina to make their plans to be away?" "That is plenty of time," announced Margaret. "About what time do you think they will be arriving? I could set out a small lunch about 1:00 if that would be okay," continued Margaret. "Morris could give them a quick tour of the grounds, and then Trisha and I will serve the lunch after another quick tour of the house." "Don't go to too much trouble," stated Sharon. "It will be no trouble at all," added Margaret.

Arthur and Gina left the manor shortly after breakfast on Wednesday. They were going to London. Gina wanted to go to the library of London history, since she had an idea of painting the manor as it was years ago, and to do that she needed to find any sources to get the placement accurate. She could ask her parents, but she wanted it to be a surprise. She would meet Jr. for lunch then go to the London archives. Arthur planned to meet Christine for lunch and then spend time with his mother and grandmother. He and Gina planned to return to the manor in time for tea. That would give Philip and his family enough time to visit the manor and the surrounding area. Of course, Arthur would call the manor before leaving London to make sure all was clear. He really

29

felt no need to meet his father. After all, Philip left when Arthur was just an infant, so would be like a stranger to him. He does not harbor any hate towards Philip, but also doesn't want to form any type of relationship with him either.

As Philip drove up to the manor along the rather long picturesque driveway, Aaron and Adam both exclaimed that the owners of the manor must be rich. Even Charlotte was amazed, as was Philip at the changes, but that it also looked like nothing seemed to have changed. It was as he remembered it, but with a difference. He was not seeing it as an English manor but rather as the place he was employed at.

When Trisha heard that the family with the two cute boys would be coming to the manor, she was excited. Now she would have a chance to talk more with the cuter one, Adam. She was hoping for a chance to get his cell number or maybe his e-mail, so they could stay in touch after they return home. Mrs. Locke noticed that Trisha was looking nervous, and asked her why. Trisha told Mrs. Locke that she found one of Philip's sons really cute and that she would like to get to know him a bit more before they go back to Canada. Well, after that Mrs. Locke couldn't resist teasing her. Even Mr. Locke teased her, with a wink.

The Locke's were waiting as they parked. Philip could tell that they had aged, but for the good. He always found that Mrs. Locke was very kind, and motherly. Mr. Locke was stern, but a very nice man, but Philip still felt nervous meeting them after all these years. Trisha was peeking out a window so she could watch the twins without them knowing. She admitted to herself that she was more nervous than she wanted to admit to the Lockes; after all, she only had a very short time to talk with them on the ferry. Maybe she was imagining the looks Adam gave her. Well, there was no better time that the present to find out, since Mrs. Locke was escorting them in and when she noticed Trisha at the window, called to her that the guests had arrived. Charlotte noticed the red cheeks on Trisha as she welcomed them. She especially noticed the look of surprise Adam gave Trisha. To Trisha's relief Mr. Locke took Philip and the twins for the tour of the grounds, while Mrs. Locke and Trisha would give Charlotte the tour of the house.

As the men were starting the tour, Aaron was teasing Adam about being in love; Adam gave Aaron a shove which in turn pushed him against Mr. Locke. An embarrassed Philip gave them a stern look, but Mr. Locke said not to worry; after all we were all boys once. No harm done.

The Lockes had agreed to meet up in the conservatory in about 45 minutes or so, for lunch.

CHAPTER

14

In London Gina enjoyed the time she was spending at the Library of London History looking into the history of her home. She was so engrossed in her research that she almost forgot that she was to meet Jr. for lunch. She must admit, she liked the feeling of just wandering around, doing whatever she pleased, even though she had her day planned.

Gina arrived at the café where she was to meet Jr. for lunch with time to spare, so she decided to sit outside and enjoy the warm sunshine. As Jr. walked up to the café, he noticed Gina sitting there with what looked like a serene smile on her face. Jr. felt so blessed to have found someone like her. She always seemed to be smiling. At that moment Gina noticed Jr. as he was walking toward her and she also felt blessed to have him in her life. "Hi, sweetheart," said Jr. as he kissed Gina on her cheek. "You look so peaceful. Are you having a good morning?" "Yes, I am," replied Gina. "I got so much information at the Library of London History, that I almost forgot that I had to meet you. I definitely will go back there in the near future." "That's good to hear," stated Jr. "I'm hungry, how about you?" "I must say, doing all that research has certainly made me hungry," answered Gina. "Let's eat." "This is delicious," stated Gina as she bit into the seafood Panini the waiter recommended. "Here, try some," she told Jr. as she passed him her plate. "You're right," observed Jr. as he took a rather huge bite. "I think I'm going to put this on the menu at home," stated Gina. "I'm sure mom and dad will love it also."

"What's your plan for after lunch"? Jr. asked. "I'm going to stop at the London Archives for a short while on my way to Arthur's grandmother's house," Gina stated. "We planned to be back at the manor in time for tea. Sometime in the near future I will return to London to continue my research at the Archives and Library of London History. There is so much there." "By the way, how is your painting coming along?" Jr. asked. "This research will be a great help to finishing it." answered Gina. "I can't wait to get home and arrange what I have." "That's great, but I must get back to the office," added Jr. "We have an important meeting with a new client. I'll be up at the manor Friday by teatime. Have a great afternoon," said Jr. as he gave Gina a kiss on the cheek before she got into a cab. "See you Friday, my love," called Gina.

Arthur's lunch with Christine had to be short, since she only had 45 minutes for lunch, but she asked her supervisor for an additional 15 minutes, promising she would stay those 15 minutes after work to finish any work that had to be completed by the day's end. Before she hurried back to her office, she kissed Arthur with the promise that she would be coming to the manor on the weekend with Jr..

Arthur walked into his grandma's feeling good. After kissing his mom, he asked where grandma was. His mom told him that she was taking a nap so as to be fully rested for his visit. "Isn't that unusual for grandma?" he asked. "Yes," stated his mom. "Your grandma has been taking naps for some time now. I convinced her to make a doctor's appointment. We will be going tomorrow." "Please call and let me know what the doctor says," stated Arthur. "I will," replied his mom. "Are you two talking about me?" asked Daphne. "Yes, grandma," replied Arthur. "I was asking mom where you were. You're looking refreshed. Maybe I should take a nap once in a while myself." "When are you leaving to return to the manor?" His mom asked. "I planned to call Mrs. Locke around 3 p.m. to make sure the coast was clear. Gina is expected to be here by then," said Arthur. "We told Mrs. Locke that we would be home in time for tea.

CHAPTER

15

During the tour Mrs. Locke was giving Charlotte, Trisha seemed to be impatient for something. Both Mrs. Locke and Charlotte knew what it was and were purposely stalling. Charlotte asked a vast array of questions from what is an airing closet to how to decide how much produce Mrs. Locke would expect from the kitchen garden, and also why is it called a kitchen garden? Mrs. Locke finally convinced Charlotte to call her Margaret. While showing Charlotte the top floor of the manor where once the servants' quarters were, Charlotte had many more questions. The floor below consisted of the nursery and a few bedrooms. Then, one floor down was the owner's bedrooms as well as a guest bedroom. Margaret brought the tour down the back stairs which the servants used. They now entered the kitchen area where there was housed the butlers' room, the housekeeper's room the laundry, and a storage room which was like a cooler, where they stored butter, preserves, fresh vegetables and fruit. Charlotte was amazed at it all. She couldn't stop saying, "Wow; I can't wait to tell my mother all about this." Lastly, Margaret showed her the area where the servants would be summoned by the mistress of the manor. Margaret pointed out the servant's bells and explained how they worked. They were for a resident who wanted to summon a servant but not have to leave the room they were in. The corresponding bell would ring and the servant would see which room the bell was indicating. "I would like a set-up like that at home," commented Charlotte. "Sometimes I am so busy and call for one of the boys but get no answer; whether they could not hear me, or not. They say they couldn't. This is amazing. It is such a huge place, how do you manage to keep up with all the housework as well as the cooking and gardening?" Since this is just a family home with only four of us living here, the work load is manageable," answered Mrs. Locke. "Thank you so much for taking time to show me around." "It was my pleasure," answered Margaret. "I rather enjoyed it. I do have help and there are only four of us living here at one time. And, I have been doing this for so long; I have it down to a science. I enjoy my work and find it very satisfying. Let's go to the conservatory, I see the men walking towards the house; they must be ready for lunch."

Charlotte turned to her sons, "Well boys, what did you think? Are you as overwhelmed as I am?" she asked. "It was nothing like I figured it would be," answered Aaron. "What did you think, Adam?" Aaron had to nudge Adam because he was busy looking at Trisha. "Oh, oh, interesting," replied a blushing Adam. "How was the tour of the house?" Philip asked Charlotte. "I had no idea what a manor house would look like; but now whenever I read a book where a manor is mentioned, I have an idea what it would look like. It was very interesting and informative," replied Charlotte. "Did you guys want a quick tour inside?" Trisha asked, as she turned to Adam. "Maybe after lunch we can squeeze it in before you leave. What do you think Mrs. Locke?" "That will be fine," Mrs. Locke replied. "Mr. Locke can take that time to give Charlotte a quick tour of the grounds. Now, who's hungry?" Trisha and Adam managed to sit next to one another where they could be heard whispering. Adam asked Trisha for her e-mail address so they could become e-mail buddies. After lunch and the quick tour of the outside for Charlotte's benefit and the inside for the boys' benefit, Philip suggested that they go and leave the Lockes to get back to their routine. Many thanks were voiced and as they drove off the Lockes went back inside while Trisha stood on the driveway staring at the retreating car. Even Buddy barked his goodbyes.

CHAPTER

16

Gina arrived at Daphne's just as Arthur was getting off the phone with Mrs. Locke. "You timed your arrival just right," stated Daphne. "Arthur was just talking to Mrs. Locke. Please fill us in, Arthur." "Mrs. Locke said that Philip and his family had left a few minutes prior to my call. And, she said we can come home now," stated Arthur. "That's wonderful," exclaimed Maggie. "But let Gina catch her breath before whisking her off. I have the kettle on, so please let's go out to the conservatory and I will bring out the tea, and Arthur, could you come and help me carry out the pastries?" "So, what did you fill your time with, Gina?" asked Daphne. "Well, first I spent an enjoyable time at the Library of London History, then after a quick lunch with Jr. I went to the London Archives. I must say, I got a lot of information and plan to return since I barely touched the surface." "What is the reason for your visits to these places?" asked Maggie as she and Arthur walked into the conservatory with the tea. "I hope to paint a series of pictures of the manor from when it was first built," explained Gina. "This will be a surprise for mom and dad, so I must insist you keep it a secret." "Don't worry," promised Daphne, our lips are sealed." "Let's enjoy our tea, because Arthur and Gina must be on their way," added Maggie.

After they cleared the busy London streets, Gina turned to Arthur and asked how his visit with Christine was. "As it was for you and Jr., our

36

lunch was short, but enjoyable. I heard you telling grandma about your visit to the Library of London History. Did you get what you needed?" Arthur asked. "Yes, I got a lot of info, but I intend to go back for another visit. There is so much more information that I didn't have time to look into," answered Gina. "And, also the Archives. Those buildings are a fountain of history. But, I have enough to get a good start."

"Do you mind if I ask how you feel about Philip's visit?" Gina queried. "If you would rather not talk about it, I understand." "I don't mind too much," replied Arthur. "You already know that Philip left when I was just an infant, and mom married Malcolm quite shortly afterwards, so to me, Malcolm is my father even though Mr. Beavington was my biological father. I don't harbor any ill feelings towards Philip."

After a short, pleasurable silence, Gina asked, "Do you remember when I brought up the subject of getting another dog?" "Yes, I do," answered Arthur. "When do you think we should get one?" "If everyone else is agreeable we could go to the dog pound in Luton this weekend. I'll bring it up at dinner," stated Gina. "I think that's a great idea," put in Arthur as he turned onto the long driveway leading up to the manor.

CHAPTER

17

Normally, Buddy would come running and barking a welcome to whomever was coming up the driveway; but today he was nowhere to be seen. Gina mentioned that fact to her father. "Buddy is in the kitchen with mom," her father told her. "He is worn out after the visit Philip and his family made." Gina looked over at Arthur raising her eyebrows. "That's something I wanted to talk about at dinner," she told her father. "It seems like Buddy needs to begin a life of luxury. I propose that we go to Luton, maybe as soon as tomorrow, and find ourselves another dog. What do you think dad?" "I agree and I know your mother would also agree. Maybe we can go for lunch then to the animal shelter," added her father.

Walking around to the back of the manor, Gina noticed her mother in the garden. "Hi, mom, do you need any help?" "I could use some," replied her mom. "My dear, Arthur and I are going out to the garage to look at a repair I was working on," stated Mr. Locke. "We will be back in time for that delicious dinner you have planned."

"Oh, I meant to ask if you think Trisha would like to come with us to Luton tomorrow," Gina asked her mom. "Normally she probably would, but she has asked to go to London for a long weekend. It seems that she has taken quite a fancy to one of Philip's sons and would like to get to know him better. They exchanged phone numbers and e-mails.

You should have seen her. She was almost tripping over herself, and your dad said the same about Adam. His twin, Aaron, was teasing him unmercifully. It was a sight," added her mom. "So, has she already left?" asked Gina. "Oh yes, just before you got home," answered her mom. "Apparently it would be a good time to visit Arthur's mother and grandmother, since she will be boarding there during her time in college." "I forgot about that," mentioned Gina. "Do you need any help with anything, mom, before I go up to my studio?" "Not at all, dear, you go ahead," replied her mom. "I'll call you when dinner is ready."

Gina had just finished making up a list of what she needed to do in her studio, when her mother called her for dinner. Time sure flew by, Gina said to herself.

"On our way home from London, I was telling Arthur about the fact that Buddy is beginning to feel his age and that maybe we should consider getting another dog," mentioned Gina. "I personally think that's a great idea," added her mom and dad simultaneously. "I suggest we leave after breakfast and run any errands, then stop for tea and pastries before going to the animal shelter," stated Gina. "Does that sound good to everyone?" After she heard their "sounds good," Gina suggested they each make a list of anything they may need apart from another leash, toys, collar and doggie dishes for their new pet. After coffee and dessert in the sun room, Mr. & Mrs. Locke excused themselves saying that it had been a busy day and they would turn in. "See you in the morning," Gina stated. "I will be turning in myself soon." "I think I'll take Buddy for a short walk before turning in myself," announced Arthur. "Goodnight everyone, come on Buddy."

18

Trisha arrived at Sharon's in time for a light tea. Sharon's mother was resting, so it was just Sharon and Trisha. During the tea they talked about the room and the commute to college. Arthur had assured Trisha that the commute was very short. Sharon showed Trisha the room and gave her a tour of the house. "You must think of our home as your own while you're here. Of course, we would expect you to pull your weight also," stated Sharon. "No need for you to worry," replied Trisha. "Mom threatened to tan my hide if I didn't help." "What are your plans for the rest of the day?" asked Sharon. "I had arranged to meet with Adam at a cafe near mom's," answered Trisha. "He's one of Philip and Charlotte's twins. He is so cute. Too bad he lives in Canada. I would like to get to know him better." "You have heard of Skype haven't you?" mentioned Sharon. "You and Adam can get to know each other that way and maybe someday he would be able to visit again, or you can visit Canada, as research about tourism in a different country." "That's great idea," stated Trisha. "How long are they staying in London?" asked Sharon. "It all depends on Philip's mother's surgery and recovery time. She should be going into hospital next week," added Trisha. "Then it will depend on how fast she recovers." "Won't Philip and his wife need to get back to Canada to jobs?" asked Sharon. "From what I understood from what Philip told Mr. Locke, he had been laid off and Charlotte wasn't working since she just had their daughter, so they have the time to stay and help his mother. The only thing would be that they miss their daughter. Charlotte's mother is looking after her," stated Trisha. "Personally, I hope their stay is long, which would give me and Adam more time to get to know each other. Neither of the twins have plans to attend college at home this fall. I must be off if I am to get to the café on time." "Enjoy," called Sharon as Trisha hurried away.

CHAPTER

19

The tram Trisha took that goes to her mother's place was late and she was worried that Adam would get tired of waiting. At the last minute she remembered that he had given her his cell phone number. When she got there, a bit out of breath, she saw him sitting at a table looking around. He is so cute, she thinks. I like his almost completely blond hair and his hazel eyes. She felt her heart jump as he spotted her and waved. "Sorry I'm late," Trisha gushes out as she tries to catch her breath. "There was a bit of a traffic jam." "No problem," answered Adam. "I just got here myself." "Do you want to sit outside in this glorious sunshine, or inside?" she asks him. "I think outside would be a good idea," suggests Adam. "This way I can people watch." "I also enjoy people watching," admitted Trisha. "You wouldn't believe what you would see. Once I saw a toddler drop a used tissue in a passing lady's shopping bag."

After they ordered, they sat in a comfortable silence, each with their own thoughts. Trisha broke the silence when their order arrived and she thanked the waitress. "How are Aaron and your parents?" she asked. "Did they enjoy the tour?" "Everyone is fine, and yes, we all enjoyed the tour. Aaron, mom and I couldn't believe that dad used to live near such a grand place and even worked there," replied Adam. "I was always in awe when we would pass the entrance way," admitted Trisha. "Can you imagine how I felt when I first got to work there? It was like a dream come true. I would imagine the residents as stuck up rich people, but I couldn't find a better, down-to-earth family than Gina and her parents. They care about the village people and treat us like we are one of them. But I have heard stories over the years that there are people who think they are better than others just because they live in such a fine place." "We also have wealthy people in Edmonton, Alberta, Canada and yes, some will stick their noses up at others," replied Adam. "I know I would never do that, because in my neighborhood there were a few guys who teased me and Aaron a lot. They had more than us, but not that much more, but they always managed to throw a snide remark at us. Aaron and I got into a few too many scuffles because of it, but nothing serious. When they heard we were going to England they were a bit put out."

"How do you like your sandwich?" Trisha asked. "It's really good. I especially like the bread," answered Adam. "They bake it fresh daily right in the restaurant," stated Trisha. "Nothing tastes better than freshly baked bread."

"Tell me about the course you will be taking this fall," asked Adam. "It's Travel and Tourism, and it's a two year course," answered Trisha. "I am so looking forward to it. I will be able to see my mother, since she lives in London. Also, I would be able to visit with my brothers; they live with our dad." "Will you be staying with your mom or at the college?" asked Adam. "I won't because mom only has a one bedroom, so Arthur's mother and grandmother said I can board with them. It is only a short tram ride to the college," replied Trisha. "How about you, what are your plans for further education?" "I haven't quite decided what I want to pursue," answered Adam. "But, I have always wanted to travel. I read a lot of books about faraway places, and can imagine myself there. What other courses does your college offer?" "I tell you what, since the college is so close we can go there and walk around the campus and take a look at some pamphlets. What do you think? Are you game?" stated Trisha. "I think that sounds like a good idea," replied Adam. "Maybe I can pick up some pamphlets on big machine engineering for Aaron."

During the walk to the college Trisha felt like she was floating on air. She enjoyed the attention Adam gave her for walking across the streets and the envious looks other girls gave her. At one point they had to get across an uneven sidewalk, so Adam took her hand and didn't let it go for a while after they safely crossed. As they were walking along, Trisha was pointing out sights that she thought would interest Adam. The questions he asked her gave her the feeling that he really was interested and was enjoying himself. Upon arrival at the college Adam picked up some pamphlets he thought would interest Aaron along with a few for himself. After a quick tour of the classes and labs, Trisha took Adam to see the dormitories. The time had passed by before she knew it, and it was time to get home. Her mother was preparing a special dinner before Trisha left to go back to the manor the next day. They walked back to the café holding hands where Adam would be able to find his way to his grandmothers. Trisha promised to call Adam before she left for the manor. He told her that he had a great time and quickly kissed her on her cheek before hurrying off. Needless to say Trisha felt she was on cloud nine and practically floated back to her mom's.

CHAPTER

20

While Adam and Trisha were getting to know each other, Philip took Aaron to a friend's garage where they work on any size vehicle, from a small scooter to a huge earth mover. The garage covered an area of about one acre. Aaron was in awe at all the different size vehicles and the large variety of tools. Philip's friend, Carlo, started working at this garage part-time during summer break, then after getting further education in automobile mechanics, he secured a full-time position. He is now a part owner. He and Philip had kept in touch with each other the entire time Philip was in Canada. Since Aaron made mention of his interest in auto mechanics, Philip asked Carlo if he could bring Aaron around for a tour. Needless to say Aaron was beside himself. He kept asking what this tool was for and that one. He could barely stand in one place wanting to look at everything. Carlo gave Aaron freedom to look around anywhere except where there was work being done on a vehicle. Then, he was allowed to look from a distance and ask questions. Before he knew it, Philip was telling him that they had to leave, that his mother was expecting them home on time for tea. With a grin as wide as the ocean, Aaron shook Carlo's hand vigorously, while gushing over his thanks. He couldn't stop thanking his father on the way home for setting up the tour. "I can't wait to tell mom and grandma all about it," gushed Aaron.

During tea, Sharon and Charlotte noticed that the twins couldn't stop smiling. Charlotte could tell that they had something on their minds. "All right, out with it," stated Charlotte as she winked at Sharon. "Judging by the smile on your face I take it that your day with Trisha went well," she mentioned as she passed the vegetables to Adam. "Yes, it did," replied Adam. "She brought me to the college where she will be attending this fall. It wasn't overly large, but it offered a lot of courses. I picked up some brochures on the tourism classes and even a few on some classes Aaron might be interested in about truck repairs and such. I have them in the bedroom and will give them to you later," Adam told Aaron. "And you, Aaron, how was your day with your dad at his friend's garage?" asked grandma. "I had a great time," gushed Aaron. "Carlo explained so much to me and even let me wander around, as long as I didn't touch anything or get in anyone's way. I have been thinking a lot about large vehicle repairs but wasn't sure I would like it. But, being at the garage, well, it was organized but a mess, if you get what I mean." "I really do understand what you're saying," replied his mother. "A mother has that feeling at the end of a hard day. Everyone is in bed, the house is clean, but not clean, do you get what I mean?" "No mom, I don't," added Aaron. "I bet your grandma does," stated his mom. "I sure do," added their grandma. "Who is ready for dessert?" As they were enjoying the delicious apple pie their grandma made, each was quiet with their own thoughts. When the adults retired to the living room with their coffee, Adam and Aaron went to their bedroom so Adam could show Aaron the brochures.

21

After breakfast, everyone armed with their lists settled in the car. Arthur had to convince Mr. Locke that it was his turn to drive, since Mr. Locke drove the last time. "I surely don't remember that," announced Mr. Locke. "You did, dear," added Mrs. Locke. "You know that you like being the driver, but you promised that next time Arthur could drive. That was so we could relax and enjoy the scenery." "You don't need to twist my arm," announced Mr. Locke. "I believe I had too much breakfast, so could use the time to just relax. I feel so stuffed."

Once they arrived in Luton, they decided to split up and each pick up whatever they had on their lists, then meet up at their favorite café for tea and snacks before going onto the animal shelter. Two hours later they were sitting in the café waiting for their orders. "Did everyone manage to procure everything on their lists?" asked Mr. Locke. "I certainly did," announced Mrs. Locke. "Plus a few more items." "What I bought will need to be picked up before we head home," stated Arthur. "Same with me," added Mr. Locke. "I got all I needed and like mom, some extras," replied Gina. "Now let's have tea."

At the animal shelter, the first dog they saw was of the same breed as Buddy. They inquired as to how long that dog had been there, whether it was a male or female, how old and if it had any health issues. The attendant was very helpful, so they took the dog for a try out in the outside area. It was a male, two years old, and well behaved. The previous owners found out that their newborn son was allergic and after trying to find a home for it themselves, as a last resort they brought it to the shelter. His name is Rusty. After several minutes of deliberation the group decided that Rusty was the dog for them. While Mr. & Mrs. Locke filled out the paper work, Gina and Arthur, along with Rusty picked out a bed, collar, leash, food bowls and a bag of treats. Mr. Locke also added a few toys. After all, he didn't think Buddy would want to share all his toys. Everyone was satisfied, even Rusty, who was wagging his tail like he was ready for takeoff. Once they got home, Mr. Locke and Arthur took Rusty out to introduce him to Buddy. Mrs. Locke went in to make a pot of tea, while Gina brought her supplies up to her studio. After about an hour, Mr. Locke announced that the two dogs got along very well. While they were having tea, they watched the dogs playing together.

Gina told her mother that she planned to go up to her studio and try to finish going through some boxes that they packed before doing the renovations on the servant's quarters. Also, there was the servant's closet of sorts that she hasn't even opened the door of. She told her mother to call her if she needed any help with dinner.

CHAPTER

22

M aggie got the call from her doctor's office to be at the hospital by 2 p.m. so they could process her for her surgery the next day. Philip and Charlotte went with her and stayed until they were chased away by the nurses. Her surgery was scheduled for 8 a.m. and with time in the recovery room; she would not be allowed visitors until at least 2 p.m. On the way home Philip showed that he was worried, which he had been advised not to do in front of his mom. Charlotte reminded him that her doctor told them it was a very short and ordinary surgery. He, himself performed one at least twice a month. After they got back to Maggie's, Charlotte made him a cuppa with some of the special biscuits he liked. Philip asked where the boys were. Charlotte told him that they went out exploring and were told to be back for tea. She suggested they go out to the conservatory to enjoy their tea while sitting amongst the beautiful flowers in peace and quiet.

"Didn't your mom ask you to call Daphne to inform her that she will be having surgery tomorrow?" asked Charlotte. "Yes, she did, since she couldn't do it herself, since her doctor called and told her that there was a cancellation and she needed to get to the hospital right away. I'll call Daphne later this evening," added Philip. "Do you still feel worried?" asked Charlotte. "I know I would, if it were my mother." "Yes, I do, even if her doctor said it was an uncomplicated procedure. I can't help it.

49

But, we must try not to show the boys that we are worried, it may just get them worried. I can see that they have come to love their grandma," added Philip. "I'm sure she will be fine," stated Charlotte. "Do you know, she asked me to pray for her?" "Thank you, dear," answered Philip, as he got up to take the tea things into the kitchen.

During dinner, the twins regaled their parents with all the sights they saw and people they met. Aaron mentioned that he found Londoners quite polite as well as helpful to lost tourists. "Oh, did you and Adam get lost?" his mother asked. "I wouldn't actually say lost, we had just taken a wrong turn. This is an interesting city. Imagine living here with all this history right around the corner." "Yes, I found it so different when I moved to Canada. I know it has its own history, but nothing like places in Europe," mentioned Philip. "Of course, people who were born here don't notice the history, or if they do, they probably don't think much about it." "There is so much to see and experience," added Adam.

"Try to get in as much sightseeing as you can before we have to go back home," announced Charlotte. "When are we leaving here?" asked Aaron. "I'm not too sure, it all depends on your grandma's recovery," answered Philip. "She will be having surgery tomorrow morning and once she has been out of the recovery room, and in another area of the hospital, her nurses will be keeping an eye out and make a record on all she does; even down to going to the bathroom. Then her doctor will be able to make a decision on when she can come home."

"Tea is ready," called Charlotte. "You two can tell us more about that wrong turn you took."

CHAPTER

23

Mr. and Mrs. Locke had both noticed how well Buddy and Rusty were getting along. As they were talking about it, Gina entered the kitchen looking for another cup of coffee before going up to her studio for a morning's work. "What's up?" she asked her parents. "We were just commenting on how well Buddy and Rusty are getting along. You would think they were long lost siblings," mentioned Mrs. Locke. "I see what you mean," stated Gina. "Just before coming down, I looked out my window and saw them playing together and then they took off like someone rang a bell, but looking further, I saw it was Arthur. He must have whistled for them. Well, I'm off to my studio, see you both later." "We have certainly been blessed in our choice of dogs," added Mr. Locke. "But, enough of this, I told Arthur I would meet him in the far field. We were talking about what to do with it." "What do you mean that you were talking about what to do with? Why do you need to do anything with it?" asked Mrs. Locke. "Mother," answered Mr. Locke. "It's to be a surprise that Arthur and Jr. are planning. I cannot say anymore. And do not tell Gina."

As soon as her father left, Gina came into the kitchen with a notebook. Her mom looked surprised. She asked Gina what it was. Gina said it was some ideas for their wedding and could she talk to her mom about them? "Sure," answered her mom. "Let's get ourselves another cup

51

of coffee and go into the conservatory." "Jr. and I have been talking and we decided we want it to be a small wedding. We want to have it in the south-east garden around 11 a.m., that way it being late August; the sun will still be shining on that area. It won't be too hot, and we always get a refreshing spring breeze there," stated Gina. "And, if it happens to rain, we can fit everyone into the dining hall." "Arthur did tell your dad that he and Christine also want a small wedding. Maybe it could be a small double wedding," replied her mom. "Yes, Jr. and I did talk about that. We plan on talking to Arthur and Christine this weekend," mentioned Gina. "Also, Jr. and I will be deciding on the invitations, as well as whatever else an engaged couple need to discuss. I brought some wedding books from the library and Christine said she also has some. It is going to be a busy weekend for us." "Don't forget I would be willing to help in any way," stated her mom. "Don't worry, I will definitely be asking for your opinion, never fear," replied Gina.

Mr. Locke and Arthur took the dogs out to the south-east corner where Arthur and Jr. had been discussing a plan they had. Arthur wanted Mr. Locke's thoughts on their plan. "Jr. and I thought that if we cleared some of these trees and made a space about the size of a soccer field, then we would build a small gazebo where the wedding ceremony would take place. For the ground, we thought of spreading very small decorative gravel, which would not require much upkeep and it would be easy on anyone walking here, as well as not being of any harm to the dog's paws," pointed out Arthur. "That sounds like a good idea," replied Mr. Locke. "Let's measure out the space and see how much work will need to be done. I guess you will want to show Jr. the area before any work is to be done." "Yes," answered Arthur. "He and Christine are coming this weekend, so while the girls are busy discussing wedding plans, Jr. and I, and you, if you wish to join us, will come out here and discuss things." "I am all for it," stated Mr. Locke. "Just a warning, I did tell Mrs. Locke that you and I were looking out here to see if we could do anything with it, but I did not mention anything else." "No problem," answered Arthur, laughing. "Mrs. Locke can try any of her wiles, but I will not talk," replied Mr. Locke. "Great," added Arthur. "I'm going to my office to draw out a plan, see you later."

CHAPTER

24

After dinner, Philip took his coffee into the sunroom to make the call to Daphne. "Hello, Daphne, it's Philip calling. Mom asked me to call you since she didn't have enough time this morning. Her doctor called and told her that there was a cancellation and she should get to the hospital as soon as possible. We left her there at about 1:45 p.m. and won't be able to see her until sometime after her surgery, which will be happening first thing in the morning. The hospital said they will call us when she is out of the recovery room." "Will you call me as soon as you can?" asked Daphne. "I will pray for her tonight." "So will we," replied Philip.

"Did you get much sleep last night?" asked Charlotte. "I know I was still awake at 1 a.m.; but I must have finally fallen asleep." "The last time I looked at the clock was shortly after 1 a.m.," replied Philip. "But it wasn't as peaceful a sleep as I would have liked." "I know what you mean," answered Charlotte. "Even though her doctor said it was not a serious surgery and that he had done many of them, I still couldn't help worrying." "I think if I can keep busy I won't worry so much," stated Philip. "Why don't we make pancakes and bacon for breakfast? I'm sure the boys will appreciate it." "Perfect," answered Charlotte.

After everyone had their fill of pancakes smothered with butter and maple syrup, Charlotte and Philip started the clean-up. After they had gotten the kitchen spic and span, they took their coffees into the conservatory and relaxed. They both must have dozed off, when they heard the phone jingling. "That must be the hospital," Philip said, as he hurried to answer it.

Maggie had just settled her mother in her favorite chair in the conservatory with her cup of late morning tea when the phone rang. "That might be Philip with a report on how Sharon is doing," she told her mom. "I won't be long." "Hello, Maggie, it's Philip, I just heard from the hospital and they told me that mom is doing fine and should be able to come home in a few days. Charlotte and I are getting ready to go see her. Shall I pass on your best wishes?" asked Philip. "That would be great, Philip," replied Maggie. "Tell her I will call in a few days and come to see her once she is settled back home. I must ring off, it sounds like something fell."

Maggie glanced in the living room but didn't see if anything in there had fallen, so she went into the kitchen. All looked okay in there. She was puzzling over what could have fallen and where, when she heard a quiet whimper. It was coming from the conservatory. She ran into the conservatory to find her mother on the floor. "Mom, mom, are you all right?" She cried. When she didn't get an answer from her mother, Maggie hurried into the kitchen to call 999. The ambulance arrived within ten minutes. The paramedics told Daphne that her mother was not responding, but was still breathing so they needed to take her to the emergency. She nodded agreement. Maggie rode in the ambulance with her.

Once they got her mother into an exam room, Maggie called Arthur's cell. She could barely compose herself to be able to tell Arthur what had happened. It turned out that Arthur was already on his way to London for a meeting. He told his mother that he would be at the hospital soon. He hurried into the waiting room and gave his mother a hug. "How is grandma?" he asked. "I don't know," answered his flustered mother. "No one has come to talk to me yet." "I'll go ask at the desk," announced Arthur. The nurse told him the doctor would be out to speak to them as soon as he could, that they should try and be patient. When Arthur got back to the waiting room he saw a man and woman talking to his mother.

"Mom, are you okay?" he asked. "Yes, yes," she stated. "I would like to introduce you to Sharon's son and daughter-in-law, Philip and Charlotte. They were visiting his mother who had surgery just yesterday. Charlotte noticed the intake of breath from Philip when he was introduced. He obviously knew who Arthur was. Before anyone could say anything else, the doctor came to talk to Maggie. Philip and Charlotte left expressing their feelings to Maggie and Arthur. Maggie in turn said she hoped Sharon would recover soon.

"How is my grandmother?" Arthur asked the doctor. "She suffered a brain aneurysm. She will be staying in hospital so we can do more tests. After that time we will know more as to what treatment she will need. There is not much more you can do here. Why don't you go home and we'll call you tomorrow after she has had more tests done." "Thank you, doctor," added Maggie. "Can we see her now?" "Just for a few minutes," cautioned the doctor. "Mom, the doctor told us that you have to stay in hospital so they can do more tests. We came to say goodnight," whispered Maggie. "The hospital will call us tomorrow once they have finished the tests. Take care, we love you."

As Maggie and Arthur were leaving, they bumped into Philip and Charlotte on their way out. Maggie told Philip to pass on her good wishes to Sharon. Charlotte added the same for Daphne

CHAPTER

25

Dorothy was sitting at the kitchen table with a letter in her hands when Trisha came in. "Hi, mom, is that another letter from your pen pal?" asked Trisha. "Yes, as a matter of fact it is," answered her mother. "She wants me to move to Calais and become a partner in her organic farming business and eatery." "Is it something you would like?" asked Trisha. "I say go for it. You only work part-time here and you love gardening and cooking, I think it's a wonderful idea. Of course, we will miss you." "I have to talk to your brothers and their father. What do you think they will say?" her mom asked. "I think they would love the idea, this way they can visit you in Calais on holidays," stated Trisha. "Even I would love to visit you on my break from classes. I will have to arrange time from any part-time job I get though. This is exciting."

After dinner and the dishes were done, Trisha went into her room to read, and then Dorothy took out the other letter she had received. It was from Henry. He encouraged Dorothy to accept her friends offer. He told her that he missed her and it would be great if she lived in Calais. Henry also said that he had been thinking about asking her to move in with him. Please think about it. Dorothy definitely had a lot to think about. She would not tell Trisha about Henry until after she was settled in Calais.

It is about one month until Trisha starts classes at Croydon College. Dorothy thinks she will wait and tell her just before that time. Dorothy

56

also has to take some time to talk to her sons and their father. She doesn't think there will be any opposition from them. Like Trisha said, the boys can visit her in Calais and she feels that they would love Calais. When Trisha leaves the next day, Dorothy planned to call Helen and discuss it with her. She really wants to go, but moving in with Henry, well, she was not sure at this time. She will wait until she has been living in Calais for some time before she makes a decision about Henry's offer. They need the time to get to know each other better. But, she is excited to have her friend Helen there.

"Do you have everything?" Dorothy asked Trisha. "Yes, I believe so," answered Trisha. "I'm on my way. See you soon. Love you." "Love you too," replied Dorothy.

Dorothy checks her address book for Helen's phone number. I hope it's not the wrong time to call her, Dorothy thinks. "Bonjour, La Petit Fleur B & B, how may I help you?" "May I speak to Helen, please?" asked Dorothy. "Dot, is that you? How are you? It's me, Helen." "Hi, do you have a few minutes to talk?" asked Dorothy. "Sure do," responded Helen "Just let me go into the office. I'm back. To what do I owe this pleasure?" "I had a letter from my pen pal asking if I would like to come to Calais and help in her restaurant. Then, I got a letter from Henry asking me to consider the offer, because he would like me to move in with him. I am so confused. What do you think?" questioned Dorothy. "Well, I know you expressed an interest in your friend's restaurant, so I don't see any reason you should not make the move. Now, the issue of Henry's question, I think you could move here and get to know him better before making a decision," replied Helen. "I'm glad you said that, it was just what I was thinking," returned Dorothy. "Great, I will answer both letters and start making arrangements. I won't leave until Trisha is in college, which is less than a month away. I'm already feeling anxious." "I'm happy for you. It will be great having you living here," answered Helen. "Let me know when you will be arriving. I must go, duty calls." "Bye," responded Dorothy.

CHAPTER

26

The doctors were very pleased with Sharon's recovery and told her she would be able to go home after the weekend. When Philip and Charlotte visited later, they were happy with Sharon's news. They had discussed that Charlotte would go home to Canada shortly after Sharon's release from hospital once Philip and the twins got used to Sharon's routine. Since the twins wanted to stay in London and Philip knew he wouldn't be able to help his mother on his own, it was decided that the twins could stay as long as they were needed. Charlotte stated that they would be helping with the housework, and cooking, while Philip would take care of any errands that needed to be done. The doctor would arrange for a home-care worker to come twice daily for a few weeks until Sharon could take care of her personal hygiene herself.

Monday morning found Charlotte putting finishing touches on Sharon's bedroom. Philip and Aaron went to pick Sharon up. Adam was relegated to going to the corner grocer for a few last minute items. Charlotte wanted Sharon's homecoming to be easy.

"It's so good to be home," sighed Sharon. "Although I understand why I had to be away for so long, but nothing is like home." "Let's get you into bed, then, I will bring you in a cuppa," announced Charlotte. "That would be heaven," said Sharon. "Philip, would you give me a hand?" asked his mother. "Where are the twins?" "They just went down to the bakery so you could have some quiet time," stated Charlotte. "They will be home for tea, of course." "While we're having tea, I will bring you up to scratch on my doctor's instructions," mentioned Sharon.

After tea, Charlotte and Philip left Sharon to have a long nap. They promised to wake her up for dinner. "Mom really looks good, after having been in hospital for two weeks," announced Philip. "Her doctor's orders don't seem too intense. And mom wants to get back to normal, so I'm sure she will follow those orders to the tee. But, we have to be sure she doesn't try to over-do it."

The twins walked in jostling each other, so Philip reminded them that grandma is home and is now resting. "What do you have there?" Charlotte asked Aaron. "We bought some of those pastries that grandma likes. Will she be allowed to have them?" stated Adam. "Yes, she can," replied his mother. "Her doctor has restricted her from having only certain foods. Those pastries are allowed. Just that she would be able to have one a day, no more."

After dinner, and enjoying a pastry the twins brought, Sharon said she was ready to turn in.

Charlotte and Philip made plans for the next day to pick up any necessary items Sharon would need, while the twins watched a suspense movie they chose.

The next day Maggie and Arthur were waiting nervously in the waiting room for the doctor. They were both sitting like in a trance. Their individual thoughts were *please don't let her die*. After all Daphne is 89 years old. She had lived a long life. Maggie now remembers the many times her mom has had to go for a nap and joked about her swollen ankles. Maggie just put it down to her mom's age, not even thinking there could be a more serious reason. She was berating herself for not insisting her mom go to a doctor. "It will be my fault if mom dies," thought Maggie.

"Mrs. Trowbridge," stated the doctor. "We confirmed that your mother does have a brain aneurysm. She fell into a coma and considering her advanced age, I am afraid she may not come out of the coma." "Oh my God, not mom," cried Maggie. "It's all my fault. I should have insisted she see a doctor when she would go for a nap each afternoon. I just thought it was a thing most seniors go through." "Mom, you can't blame yourself," comforted Arthur. "How were you to know? Even I noticed that she rested more frequently and I didn't say anything." "No one is to blame, Mrs. Trowbridge," mentioned the doctor. "It is natural for someone her age, thinking it's just that they are older and that is why they take naps. You cannot blame yourself." "Can we see her?" asked Arthur. "Just for a short while," responded the doctor. A nurse will have to stay in the room while you are there, just for precautionary reasons." The doctor's phone beeped. After looking at it, he excused himself and hurried away. Maggie and Arthur decided to go visit Daphne. As they arrived at her room, there was a flurry of activity. Doctors and nurses were hurrying in and out of Daphne's room. Maggie gasped and seemed about to pass out. Arthur guided her to a seat. Daphne's doctor came out of her room and approached Maggie. "I'm terribly sorry, Mrs. Trowbridge. We did all we could. Your mom has passed away." Maggie burst out in tears while Arthur looked stunned. "I'm sorry," stated the head nurse. "You may sit with her for a short while." "Thank you, nurse," responded Arthur, as he guided his mother to the bedside. Maggie continues crying and had trouble accepting her mother's passing.

"Come on mom, I'll take you home and make us a cuppa," stated Arthur. "Yes, sure," answered his mom." She didn't really hear what he said. She was in shock. Once Arthur got his mom settled with a cup of tea, he went to the lounge and called the manor. Mrs. Locke answered and after hearing the news, she had to sit down. Mr. Locke asked, "What's the matter?" He took the phone from her and continued talking with Arthur. Gina walked into the kitchen shortly after Mr. Locke hung up the phone and seeing her parents looking shocked, she got worried and asked her mom what was the matter. Mr. Locke gently told her that Arthur's grandmother had just passed away.

Arthur was waiting for Christine to come home and then the three of them were just going to have a quiet night. He continued to make funeral plans the next day. He would call us with the details as soon as everything was finalized.

28

Gina had come into the kitchen to tell her mom about the wedding plans she and Jr. had made. But, after hearing the sad news, she put that on hold. She went to her office to call Jr. with the news.

Mr. and Mrs. Locke were devastated by the news. They had known Daphne since they were in grade school. Daphne and her husband lived in Dumforton as did Mr. Locke. Mr. Locke went to school with Maggie. Mrs. Locke grew up in Luton. They met at a multi-school event that was held in Luton when they were in their early teens. They kept up a long distance friendship even though they didn't live too far apart. After high school, they both went to different colleges in London and lost touch. As fate would have it, they met up again at an event for alumni for their school district.

Mrs. Locke was all for going to London to offer any help, but Mr. Locke suggested that they give Maggie and Arthur some time alone to grieve and that they should wait for Arthur to call regarding the funeral details. Needless to say their evening meal was solemn.

After their meal they each went their separate ways, understanding the others need for private grieving.

CHAPTER

29

Sharon's doctor was very pleased with the progress she had made so far in her recovery. It was good news for everyone. That evening after dinner, Sharon, Philip and Charlotte discussed the future. Sharon agreed that Charlotte should go back home to be with their daughter. Philip and the twins would stay longer. "If all goes well," stated Sharon, "It won't be too long before you are all reunited in Canada. Although; I will miss you terribly. By the way, I overheard the twins talking about staying in London and taking courses at Croydon College. Have they said anything to either of you?" "No, but I do know that Aaron enjoyed his visit to Carlo's garage," mentioned Philip. "And I noticed how excited Adam was when he was talking about his visit to the college Trisha will be attending, and that he brought some brochures home about the tourism course," stated Charlotte. "Do you think they were serious?" "I would say they haven't been so excited about much in the past. This visit has been good for them. They should thank you mom, for needing our help," added Philip. "If they bring up the subject of those brochures again soon, I would assume it means a lot to them. We'll wait and see, but don't wait too long."

When the twins returned, Charlotte and Philip took the time to go out for some personal sightseeing. Sharon and the twins decided to have some pastries in the conservatory. "Boys, I must confess that I overheard the two of you talking about hoping to stay in London to attend Croydon College," announced Sharon. "Have you told your parents?" "No," stated Aaron. "They would tell us that they couldn't afford it, which is probably true. Dad hadn't been able to find another job after being let go; but it came at just the right time. You wrote him and here we are." "If your first year of tuition could be paid, would you want to stay?" asked Sharon. "You would be able to stay here, therefore saving on dorm fees. And, you could work during summer to save up for the next year's tuition. After all, the courses are only for two years, right?" "That sounds like a dream come true," stated Adam. "Would you talk to them for us?" "No," replied Sharon. "We can all talk to them together, right after tea; I think that would be a good idea."

"How was your sightseeing, Charlotte?" asked Sharon. "I am amazed at the history of most buildings. I will have a lot to tell my mother and friends when I get home. Part of me doesn't want to leave, but I do miss Annabelle so much; and it was wonderful getting to know you," stated Charlotte.

"I have something I would like to talk about with you regarding the twins," announced Sharon. "They told me that they would love to take some courses at Croydon, but that you wouldn't be able to afford their tuition." "Yes, that's true," replied Philip. "You know that I lost my job and couldn't find another one. Charlotte and I would like for the twins to stay and immerse themselves in a different culture, but as you said, we cannot afford the tuition." "But, if their first year tuition was paid, would you let them stay?" asked Sharon. "They would be able to live here, thereby saving on dorm fees, and they could work over the summer break to save for the next year. If I am remembering correctly, they may be able to apply for a grant, for foreign students. What do you think? Should we look into it?" "Please mom, dad," begged the twins. "Can we do it? Please," "We'll definitely think about it," answered Philip. "But where would we get the money to pay for the first year?" "I would pay it," announced Sharon. "I have my investments, plus a pay-out from my last place of employment. It will be more than enough." "Are you sure?" questioned Charlotte. "Have you thought this through?" "I am positive," answered Sharon. "Like I said," stated Philip. "We will think about it. Now I see you are tired, mother, it's time you turned in."

30

Maggie, Arthur and Christine's tea started out somber, but soon they were remembering funny things Daphne would say and how she was always there to help anyone. Maggie remembered that her mother would always be one of the first to volunteer at a church function and insist Maggie tag along. Soon they were chuckling over many of Daphne's antics. By the time they settled in the conservatory for after dinner tea and dessert their moods were lighter. Even though Christine had only met Daphne about four years ago, she still was able to make mention of a few instances where Daphne made her laugh and comforted her, especially after her mother's passing. Needless to say, Maggie went to bed feeling better and she was able to say she slept like a baby.

Arthur and Christine stayed up and talked more about their experiences with Daphne. Arthur admitted that if it weren't for his grandmother, he wasn't sure how he and his mother would have survived on their own.

Arthur told Christine after she leaves for work tomorrow, he and his mom will make the funeral arrangements. As per his grandmother's wishes, it will be a small affair. Arthur remembered the day his mom, grandmother and he talked about funeral wishes. Arthur admitted that he thought it wasn't a topic he would pick to talk about, but after the passing of a good friend of his grandmothers, she made mention of her wishes. At first he didn't want to hear it, but knowing his grandmother, he had a change of mind and listened while her plans were talked about. Actually, his grandmother had Maggie write out those plans and keep them in an important place for safekeeping. After all, his grandmother stated, you never know when the Good Lord is going to call you home.

Surprisingly, everyone had a peaceful sleep that night.

After Christine left for work, Arthur and his mother took their last cup of tea into the conservatory. Maggie had brought the list she made by the request of Daphne. Daphne wanted only very close family and a few friends. After all many of her friends were either home-bound or had already passed away. They were to have her favorite flowers, Chrysanthemums, in as many colors as they could get. There were also a few of her favorite hymns to choose from. Her solicitor was invited, not only because he was her solicitor, but he was also a good friend.

Maggie contacted the local bakery to order some of her mother's favorite pastries. The church has enough room and equipment for tea and coffee making. Once the day was decided, Maggie and Arthur continued to call people, advising them of the time and place. It was to be held four days from then. The only people who would be coming from afar were the Lockes.

After the arrangements were made, Maggie excused herself and went into her mother's bedroom, where she sat on the bed and cried. Arthur heard her as he was passing, but did not interrupt. He felt like crying himself.

The day of the Celebration of Living for Daphne was sunny and not too warm. The time to be spent at the graveside would be ideal. Daphne loved sunny days. During the reception later, there were many tears as well as laughs. Maggie remembered her mother telling her that she was born on a sunny, warm day.

The Locke's and Jr. returned to Maggie's home after the celebration. The solicitor would be meeting them there. Daphne had left Maggie quite comfortable and bequeathed a considerable amount on Arthur as well. She also insisted in her instructions that Arthur and Christine should carry on with their wedding plans as previously decided.

Daphne was a woman who will not soon be forgotten.

CHAPTER

31

While driving home the Locke's continued to reminisce about Daphne. Gina sat in the back seat engrossed in her own thoughts. The solicitor mentioned that Daphne had insisted that they should continue with their wedding plans. Gina told her parents that she and Jr. will be discussing their plans when Jr. comes up on the weekend. Arthur had told her that he and Christine will be doing the same.

The next morning things were back to normal, but lacking their usual "it's a great day" attitude.

As what sometimes happens when an older friend passes away, the survivors also think about their time left on earth. They plan to get their house in order either by having a will made up or making changes to their existing will. It is a time for reflection.

During breakfast each person mentioned their plans which involved being alone. Mr. Locke said he would take the dogs for a stroll into the woods, Mrs. Locke wanted to do some baking, and Gina stated that she will go up to her office to get some work done. Each person respected each other's wishes.

When they met for lunch, their conversations were about what their plans would be for the remainder of the day. For Gina, it was wedding plans, for Mr. Locke, it was cleaning up the garden beds after the recent rain they had, and for Mrs. Locke, it was airing out the linen closets.

The dogs wandered around but regularly came to where Mr. Locke was working. They sensed something had happened. Mr. Locke trimmed the rose bushes that the Beavingtons brought back from one of their trips. Mrs. Locke mentioned that she would like to make a few bouquets for the dining room on the wedding day, depending on the choice of flowers Gina and Christine wished. They could always go on a side table. She knew that Gina and Christine had already discussed baby's breath for decorating the mantle on the Inglenook fireplace. The choice of colors has not yet been determined. By the time Mrs. Locke called them in for dinner; each person had been focused on their individual tasks and was ready for sharing on how their day had gone. For now and a long time yet, sadness would creep up at any time during their days.

For the reception dinner, Gina and Christine had been e-mailing each other regularly and they will finalize the menu and flower type and colors this coming weekend.

Next day, Arthur and Christine arrived just minutes before Jr. After hugs all around Mrs. Locke ushered everyone into the conservatory for a late lunch of a green salad, cheese and a plate of cold cuts along with fresh bread. She had also made a strawberry torte for dessert.

After the lunch, the two couples went out to the gazebo to continue with wedding plans. Since there will be no Maids of Honors or Groomsmen, choosing the flower colors would be just a matter of personal choice. Together, Gina and Christine decided on blush which is one of Gina's favorites and a raspberry color, (which was the main color in the McGregor clan's tartan) and baby's breath to decorate the Inglenook fireplace. The orange and yellow roses from the garden would look wonderful in vases on the corner tables as well as the sofa side table.

The next morning, Gina, Christine and Mrs. Locke drove to London to do the final fittings on their wedding dresses. After they stored the dresses and other accessories in the boot of the car, they took some time to visit Maggie before returning home. She left instructions with Mr. Locke and the boys for having the dinner ready for when they arrived back at the manor. Mr. Locke agreed with her decision because he felt that the ladies would be exhausted after the trip to London and the visit with Maggie. He reassured Mrs. Locke not to worry that all will be ready upon their return.

Maggie was pleased to see Mrs. Locke and the girls. After hugs and some tears, they retired to the conservatory for tea and pastries. Maggie had just made a fresh batch of scones.

To delay having to talk about her mother, Maggie asked the girls how their wedding plans were going. "We have the dresses in the boot, along with accessories," stated Gina. "Have you chosen your colors?" asked Maggie. "Yes, we have," announced Christine. "We plan to have baby's breath decorating the Inglenook fireplace in the colors of blush for Gina and raspberry for me." "Oh, why raspberry?" questioned Maggie. "Raspberry is the main color of the McGregor's clan tartan." "And mom will set a few vases of roses from the garden onto the side tables," added Gina. "Our bridal bouquets will be white roses with the blush and raspberry baby's breath added." "What about the menu, do you have it already planned?" asked Maggie. "We will be having cucumber sandwiches and a vegetable platter with cheese. We will be using vegetables from our garden," stated Mrs. Locke. "There will also be a cold cuts platter." "For dessert, we have chosen strawberry tarts and a Scottish pudding, called Cranachan using raspberries from the garden," added Gina. "What is Cranachan pudding?" asked Maggie. "It consists of oats, cream, raspberries and whiskey," stated Christine. "Plus, mom and Christine will make some Scottish tea cookies, added Gina." "For beverages, we will have tea, coffee, and lemonade. There will be wine for the final toast," continued Mrs. Locke. "It sounds like you have everything decided," mentioned Maggie. "What about music? Have you booked a band?" "We did book a trio," answered Gina. "The manager at the dog pound gave us a name of a trio of two men and a woman. Christine and I had them audition and they just grabbed at our hearts."

As they were leaving Maggie turned to Mrs. Locke and told her to call if she needed any help with anything.

The next day, Sharon and the twins went to the college to find out about applying for a scholarship grant. They were welcomed by an admissions assistant and were able to fill out some applications, and were sent home with some forms their parents needed to fill out. The assistant mentioned that the sooner they brought the forms back, the sooner they would hear if they were successful in receiving a grant. The twins were very excited about the possibility of staying in London. They couldn't thank Grandma Sharon enough on their way home.

When they got home, Philip asked how things went. "The admissions assistant was very helpful," stated Sharon. "We have some information you need to read and then the forms that you both need to fill out. The assistant mentioned that the sooner we bring the forms back, the sooner the boys will hear back." Philip turned to the boys, and told them that after dinner he and their mother will read all the information and fill out the forms. "Thank you so much," added Aaron. "Maybe you and mom can come with us to the college tomorrow when we return the forms." "I think that would be a great idea," announced Charlotte.

After the forms were filled out and ready to be returned, Philip and Charlotte told his mom and the twins that they would be going back to Canada next week. "We miss your little sister very much," mentioned their mom. "We will definitely be in touch with you so we can hear all your good news. I am certain that you will both receive a grant." "I hope so," stated Adam. "I really like London, and being able to further my education out of Canada is not what many people can say. Aaron and I are blessed to have such a wonderful grandmother who is willing to help us with such an opportunity." "I don't know about you boys, but I'm tired after all this excitement, I'm going to turn in early," stated grandma. "See you all in the morning."

The next morning, Adam and Aaron decided to make breakfast for their parents and grandmother. They were very anxious to return the forms to the college. "What a wonderful treat," mentioned a surprised Sharon. "I won't be going with you and your parents to the college; yesterday was a very tiring one for me. I will patiently wait to hear your news when you get home. I plan on making a special tea for tonight." After much fidgeting, Philip told the twins that he and their mother were ready to go to the college.

Adam had called Trisha after tea last night and told her the good news. He and Aaron are excited about the possibility of attending college and living in London. Trisha wished them good luck. They arranged to meet later the next day to exchange news. Trisha told Adam she also had some news.

At the college the admissions assistant had very good news for the twins. Apparently, two applicants backed out leaving space for two new applications for grants. The grant committee would be meeting the following day to decide which applicants would be offered the available grants. The assistant was very confident that the twins would be successful in receiving a grant. They all went home full of hope.

Adam met Trisha as arranged and couldn't wait to tell her his great news. She commented on his big smile. "We were advised that the chances of receiving a grant are quite high," Adam told Trisha. "Two earlier applicants backed out so Aaron and I have our fingers crossed." "That's great news," replied Trisha. "Be sure to call me as soon as you hear." "I certainly will," replied Adam. "You said you also had some good news, tell me." "Do you remember I told you that my mom has a pen pal in Calais? Well, her pen pal needs her to help with her B & B, and mom decided to leave London right before the weddings at the manor.

I had visited there once and would love to go over for holidays or just for a long weekend. My brothers are also excited about that prospect." "That is good news for sure," added Adam. "When we went to Calais, we had a good time, but didn't stay very long, so it would be interesting to go again. Should we get one of the grants, I may be able to squeeze in the odd visit or two. It's going to be a long night, hoping that the college will call tomorrow. Their meeting is set for 9 a.m. We will be on pins and needles."

33

After tea the two couples took their coffees out to the conservatory to discuss the wedding plans. "OK," announced Gina. "The invitations have been sent out; we have the dresses and accessories; the menu has been finalized as well as the flowers.

Now we need to discuss the guests and their accommodations." "My father and brothers would be staying at the manor from the day before and for a few days after," stated Christine. "Trisha and Arthur's mom will be staying at Dorothy's cottage in Cockernhoe, which is close enough for Trisha to come over in the morning," added Gina. "DS Dunes and Liz will just come for the day since they have a toddler and Liz is expecting her second child in about a couple of months." "My parents can stay at my place and come to the manor on the morning of the wedding. After the wedding they are planning to stay in London to visit friends while Gina and I are away on our honeymoon," mentioned Jr.. "Gina and I will stay at my parents' home in Coudekerque-Branche, France and use it as a base while we tour around that area for the ten days we will be gone." Arthur piped up, "Christine and I will stay at mom's for the night then continue driving toward Scotland, stopping for a night here and there. We will arrive at Kirkcudbright about the same time Christine's family arrive back home. Christine will be my tour guide in her home town."

"I think that about covers everything," Gina stated. "If anyone thinks of anything I might have missed, please let me know." "Here comes mom and dad with more coffee and dessert."

"Do you have everything finalized?" asked Mrs. Locke. "Yes, I believe so, we were just discussing guests and accommodations," answered Gina, "But if you can think of anything we may have missed, please let me know."

"Just to confirm about Christine's family coming for the engagement dinner," mentioned Gina. "Since it's a school break, they would have the time to drive up one day, the dinner will be the following day, and the last day they are driving back to Scotland. Christine called her father and he agreed to the plans. They won't have much time to visit, but they will be staying longer when they come for the wedding."

"Is that strawberry rhubarb pie I smell?" announced Jr. "It sure is," stated Mr. Locke, "and I brought ice-cream along for those who may want it." Both Jr. and Arthur raised their hands, and said, yes please.

The rest of the evening was passed in pleasant conversation. Gina brought up the fact that Buddy was really starting to show his age. "I noticed Rusty has been staying with Buddy as he naps and that Buddy hasn't been eating as much, so I made an appointment with the vet for Monday," announced Mr. Locke. "Your mom and I will pick up a few things after the vet visit and fit in a tea break. Let your mom know if you need anything."

34

Adam and Aaron were elated when they heard that they succeeded in obtaining a grant. It would be a full grant which meant all their fees and books, etc. would be paid for for the full two years. They would also receive a partial stipend for living expenses; such as meals or travel expenses, but, since they would be staying with their grandma they would be able to save the meal allowance. It meant that they wouldn't have to be in any hurry or even have to find part-time jobs. Their parents advised them that they should focus on their studies for the first six months to see how intense their workloads would be.

After the twins completed their admission forms they received their college passes and were advised not to lose them, but they could be replaced if lost, for a small fee. Along with their passes they received their book list and with their parents trailing along, the twins were able to purchase all their books and any other supplies they would need. Laden with several packages, their parents took the boys out for some tea and scones before heading home. Charlotte didn't want to leave Sharon too long on her own.

When they got home, the twins talked their grandma's ears off showing her their books and supplies. Philip and Charlotte told each other that they had not seen their sons so excited about anything for a long time. After a short while, Philip came into the conservatory to rescue his mom; she was looking tired.

Philip went into the study to "check his e-mails" (or so he told Charlotte). He actually wanted to apply for a job that he noticed was posted at the college. It was for the exact type of work he did while working at the manor as a young man. He wanted to keep it a secret, in case nothing came from it. Aaron also went off to e-mail a friend in Canada about his plans, while Adam called Tricia. They agreed to meet the next day. Adam was so excited about the fact that he would be able to continue his friendship with Tricia and she couldn't wait to tell her mother. At least both of them would have someone they knew on campus, so they wouldn't feel alone.

The next day Charlotte and Philip bought Charlotte's ticket to go back to Canada. She would be leaving in two days' time. She wanted to go with Sharon and the twins on their shopping trip. Sharon insisted on buying them some new clothes.

After tea, Charlotte and Philip were treated to a fashion show. The twins modeled their new outfits. "Now you both look British," stated Sharon. "You both look handsome," announced Charlotte. "I'm proud of both of you." "Grandma also bought Annabelle a few items," added Aaron. "Do you think you can squeeze them in your suitcase?" "I certainly will, along with the few other items I bought mother," stated Charlotte. "Thank you so much, Sharon. I will take pictures of Annabelle in them and send you the pictures."

"After I pack tomorrow, your father and I are going out for dinner, alone," announced Charlotte. "You boys and grandma will be on your own."

Once Charlotte's flight left, Philip had to hurry back to town; he had an interview to get to. It was a short interview. The employers had Philip wait in the reception area while they discussed his application. After only twenty-five minutes, they called him back into the office and offered him the job. The next day he had to be at the college to meet the rest of the team. There was a lot of landscaping for them to work on before classes started September 3. The official day of work would be August 2. The twins and Sharon were so happy for him. That would give him time to fly back to Canada to help Charlotte pack their house. Thank goodness they were only renting. He had to wait until he knew Charlotte was home before he could call her to tell her the good news.

"We plan to have the engagement dinner April 22. That way it would give Christine's father time to arrange for those days off work," announced Arthur. "There are no classes for the boys since it's a bank holiday. They can stay the weekend at the manor. Again, thank you Mrs. Locke for agreeing to that plan." "They will also be staying here at the manor for the wedding, won't they?" asked Mrs. Locke. "Yes, her father has already booked that week off. "Would your father's employer be okay with him booking a longer holiday for the wedding?" Mrs. Locke asked Christine. "Oh yes, dad has some banked holiday time, so it will not be a problem, since our wedding is August 27, that gives his employer sufficient notice," added Christine. "The first night they can stay at moms, and then they can drive to the manor together with Christine," stated Arthur. "Christine feels that her brothers would enjoy the longer stay here. Mr. Locke agreed to let them follow him around."

"What is the menu going to be?" Gina asked her mom. "Since our chickens are lying very well, I decided on a vegetable quiche, with pepper, onion, zucchini, mozzarella cheese, and maybe mushrooms. I already asked if anyone was allergic to any of those ingredients," added Mrs. Locke. "I will also have a green salad and dinner rolls. For dessert I will make another strawberry rhubarb pie and the much loved apple pie.

What do you think of my choices?" "That sounds splendid," stated Gina and Christine simultaneously.

"Trisha and her mom plan to be here for the dinner, won't they?" Mr. Locke asked. "Yes," added Gina. "They will stay at the cottage in Cockernhoe, but have offered to help with anything we need done." "I do admire how Dorothy had raised Trisha," added Mrs. Locke. "She enjoys helping people so I know she will do very well in her course."

"How is your mother doing?" asked Mrs. Locke. "Is she up to joining us for the dinner so soon after Daphne's passing?" "Mom is fine," stated Arthur. "It was grandma's final wish that we carry on with our wedding."

CHAPTER

36

After his phone call to Charlotte, Philip went to purchase his ticket home. Meanwhile, Charlotte would start packing and deciding what they would really need. They would purchase whatever was necessary since it would be less expensive than shipping things overseas. Sharon told them they can stay with her, since the time they had been there, they had enough room, but Philip mentioned that their daughter will be coming back with them. Adam brought up the fact that he and Aaron have full scholarships that entailed boarding at the college. They still had time to go to the college and arrange for a room that the registrar mentioned. That would leave their room available for Annabelle.

Until classes started, Aaron got a part-time job at Carlo's garage. It just consisted of sweeping, collecting the garbage and general clean-up, but he felt he was on cloud 9. He was scheduled Monday, Wednesday and Friday's from 11 a.m. 'til 3 p.m. He stayed after his shift for a short while just watching the other technicians. Adam also got some work helping at the nearby grocer, bagging groceries, and performing carry out duties. He even helped stock shelves. This way they both felt they were not being burdens on their parents. What with the flights back and forth to Canada, they felt they needed to be very careful of their spending until their dad received his first paycheque. Also, Sharon was giving them some cooking tips, and told them that they would be welcome to come

79

home for dinners whenever they wished. For sure they would be coming for Sunday dinners, if they didn't have exams looming.

Sharon's doctor was very pleased with her recovery after her surgery. But, he had cautioned her not to overdo it just because she feels good. For someone her age, her doctor said, the body would need more time to recuperate. "Be sure to contact my office if you feel anything out of the ordinary," stated her doctor. "I sure will," replied Sharon. "I don't want to go through what I did before, and now I have my son and his family home, I want to be around to enjoy them for many years." "That's the spirit, a positive attitude breeds positive living," announced her doctor.

Later that day, when the twins came home they found their grandma humming while cooking dinner. "Did you win the lottery, grandma?" Aaron asked. "Oh, no," replied grandma. "I had a good visit with my doctor. He said I am almost as good a new, but I must pace myself." "Don't worry, grandma," stated Adam. "We will be here for you." "Thank you boys," answered Sharon with tears in her eyes. "I never thought I would be blessed with two such caring grandsons. Give your grandma a hug then go wash up for dinner."

After dinner Adam checked his e-mail and found one from his father for his grandma. The three of them read it together. Philip and Charlotte decided to pack a crate about 6 feet by 6 feet. They were advised that the one crate would cost slightly less than individual boxes. And, whatever they couldn't pack, they would have a garage sale, and donate what won't sell. Apparently, the college issued Philip a moving allowance that would help with the expenses. So, if all went well, Philip, Charlotte and Annabelle would depart Canada within two weeks.

CHAPTER

37

❦

The day had arrived for the engagement dinner. Mrs. Locke rose early to make sure she had everything they needed. She was busy making a list for Mr. Locke to pick up last minute items when he walked into the kitchen. "Don't worry, mother," put in Mr. Locke. "Everything will be fine." "You don't understand, father," replied Mrs. Locke. "This is our daughter's engagement dinner, she will only get engaged once in her lifetime. I want it to be a night she won't forget as well as Christine." "I do know Gina and Christine would not want you to get stressed out," added Mr. Locke. "Please relax and breathe. Didn't Dorothy and Trisha say they would be here to help?" "Yes they did and you're right, father," added Mrs. Locke as she sat down. "What would I ever do without you?" "I feel the same, my dear," replied Mr. Locke as he gives her a quick kiss on the cheek. "Now, hand me your list and I will be off." "Be sure not to lollygag around," stated Mrs. Locke.

Gina was up in her room trying to decide what to wear to the dinner. Her mom said it was casual, so just about anything would be fine. She finally decided on a summer dress that Jr. had once complemented her on early in their relationship. I wonder if he would even remember it, Gina asked herself.

Little did Gina know that Christine also was wondering what to wear. She finally decided on a spring dress with tiny raspberry colored

81

flowers on it. She was in a rush because her father and brothers were expected to arrive any time. She wanted to be ready to head out to the manor as soon as they had a few minutes to stretch their legs. Arthur and his mother had already left, in case Mrs. Locke might need some help.

Christine's brothers were really happy to see her. They kept asking where the manor was. Their father had to shush them so he could concentrate on driving. Upon arrival at the manor, the brothers were awestruck. They had no idea what a manor would look like, even though there are such homes in Scotland. The fact that their sister would be living in one made it extra special. Buddy and Rusty welcomed the boys with wagging tails and acted like they were already family and hadn't seen them in a long time.

After hugs from her father and brothers, Christine introduced Mr. and Mrs. Locke. "Dad, "I would like to introduce you to Alicia's parents, Morris and Margaret Locke. Mr. & Mrs. Locke, this is my father Angus and my brothers, Duncan and Cameron," "It's nice to meet you Mr. & Mrs. Locke," mentioned Angus. "Please, we are almost family, so please call us Morris and Margaret," announced Mr. Locke. "You'll meet the others at the luncheon," Christine mentioned to her father. After Christine showed them to their rooms, Mr. Locke took them on a tour. With the excitement of the boys, together with the excitement of the dogs, it was a noisy tour.

Trisha and her mother came to help prepare the luncheon. Dorothy and Maggie had some time to catch-up at that time. Trisha was sent out to tell everyone that Mrs. Locke had luncheon ready. It consisted of cold cuts, cheese, crackers, fruit and tea or coffee and lemonade for the boys. After they ate, Arthur and Christine took her father on a special tour outlining plans Arthur and Gina had for the manor. Trisha took Christine's brothers out for a walk in the woods with the dogs. Since the dinner wouldn't be served for another 3 hours, Mrs. Locke, Maggie and Dorothy went to the conservatory with a cup of tea to put their feet up. The afternoon seemed to fly by. Next thing they knew, Mr. Locke had come into the conservatory to remind Mrs. Locke of the time.

Jr. arrived with just minutes to spare before Mrs. Locke called everyone in for dinner. He had to pick up a gift he and Gina decided to buy for her parents for agreeing to have the dinner at the manor.

Everyone complemented Mrs. Locke on the fine dinner. The conversation was varied. Mr. Locke was kept busy answering questions from Christine's brothers, while Christine's father and Arthur were discussing some of the plans for the manor. Gina and Jr. had time only for each other. All in all, it was a successful evening. Christine's brothers went to bed without any complaints, but only if they would be able to walk the dogs before going to bed. Arthur and Christine went for the walk with them. Gina kissed her parents thank you then she and Jr. went for a short walk before turning in. Once the kitchen was put to rights, Mrs. Locke and Maggie also turned in. Mr. Locke was the last one to retire after he locked all doors.

On their way back to Cockernhoe, Dorothy was telling Trisha that her pen-pal asked her if she would move to Calais and help at the B & B. Dorothy told Trisha that she decided to go. "I'm happy for you, mom," replied Trisha. "It must have been a hard decision." "The timing was right," mentioned Dorothy. "You're going to college, and your brothers are settled with their father, and, it's only a short ferry ride away. I'm hoping you can visit when you have class breaks. I will also tell your brothers the same." "When do you leave?" asked Trisha. "I already put in my notice to my landlord and boss," stated Dorothy. "It's just a matter of packing." "I'll help in any way I can," added Trisha. "I love you, mom." "And I love you," Dorothy said, as she gave Trisha a hug. "Come on, let's go to bed, I'm tired."

38

With the arrival of Philip, Charlotte and Annabelle, Sharon was as happy as a lark. She took over the care of Annabelle while Philip and Charlotte unpacked their few belongings. The twins went through their stuff to decide what they would take to their college dorm. Sharon was kept busy with little Annabelle, who was crawling quite well. Philip would be starting work in a couple of months. Firstly, they had to go out and buy Annabelle a bed, since it would have cost more to ship her existing bed. Sharon told them of some bargain shops where they could find just about anything they would need. Philip and Charlotte were successful in purchasing a baby bed and sheets to fit. The bed they bought could be transformed into a child's bed as Annabelle grew. After buying a few more toys, Annabelle's room was just right.

Sharon's home took on a new schedule. The twins would go to work, and Philip would work on any repairs he saw needed to be done, while Sharon and Charlotte reorganized the rooms. Sharon decided that Charlotte and Philip would have the bigger bedroom and she would take the bedsit downstairs. Once Philip and the twins had moved Sharon's belongings downstairs, Charlotte decided to clean the upstairs bedroom before asking Philip to bring in their belongings. The twins would occupy the room their parents had, until they move into the dorm; that room would be for company or whenever the twins decided to spend a night;

or also on school breaks. The room they had occupied will be set up for Annabelle. Sharon enjoyed being kept busy keeping Annabelle occupied.

Before they knew it, August had arrived and Philip started work. He told Charlotte and his mother that he felt it very relaxing working with plants. In no time he had remembered a lot of what he learned when working at the Manor. Sharon's doctor appointments were good news. Her doctor was very pleased with her recovery. Also, Charlotte made some new few friends when she took Annabelle for a stroll in the nearby park.

Adam and Aaron would be moving into their campus dorm in the last week of August, since classes would be commencing the following week. It also would give students a chance to walk around the college to orientate themselves so as not to get lost the first week. Adam called Trisha to meet him in the college rotunda for a break during the move. They decided to walk around campus together to check out where certain areas were. Aaron had met one of their dorm neighbors who invited him to go to the nearest café for some delicious muffins. The college café would not open for another couple of days.

"Are you excited that your parents and sister will be living in London?" Trisha asked Adam. "Yes, I am," replied Adam. "I didn't realize how much I missed Annabelle until I saw her again. She really has grown. She's crawling around everywhere. We have to watch where we walk. Did I tell you that dad got a job here at the college?" "No, I don't think so, but good for him," answered Trisha. "What will he be doing?" "He will be part of the landscaping team. We might even see him working on the grounds from time to time," Adam stated.

"How are things with you?" Adam asked Trisha. "I must say that I am going to be very busy this next month," she replied. "My mom told me that she will be moving to Calais to help her pen-pal in her B & B. business. She had planned to leave in mid-August, to be there to help her friend with the next long weekend rush," replied Trisha. "I would be able to go there during a college break, even if it's just for two or three days. I can always study there for any upcoming exams. I'm happy for my mother." "Are you all settled in Arthur's mother's place?" questioned Adam. "Not yet," answered Trisha. "Mom said she would help me decorate my room. Arthur's mother gave me permission to make any changes I want, apart from tearing any walls down. Then I'm going to see mom off at the ferry. Also, I will be attending the weddings at the manor."

"Have you looked over your class schedule yet?" Trisha asked. "I'm glad we're taking the same course. Maybe we can study together. What do you think?" "I think that would be great," replied Adam. "Maybe we can form a study group for one night a week and the other nights if we can, I would love to have you as my study partner." "I never thought I would be so excited about school," stated Trisha.

CHAPTER

39

Gina had some spare time on her hands so she decided now would be the best time to tackle that small room up in the servant's quarters. It's been 3 years. She just hadn't found the time. She changed into some grubby clothes and went in. It was a rather small room, only about 6 feet by 4 feet. The servants had probably used it for storage. It smelled of a room that had been closed in for many years. Gina was relieved to notice that there was a light switch. Turning on the light she noticed many spider webs, which she brushed aside. She was then able to take in the condition of the room. It had wood floors and was covered in wall paper in a butterfly pattern which had peeled in many places. When it was new, the wall paper would have brightened up the room. The floors looked in good condition except one place that squeaked quite a bit when Gina walked around the room. She was just about to examine that floor further when she heard her father calling her for dinner. Where did the time go? she asked herself as she went to her room to change out of her dusty clothes.

During dinner, Mrs. Locke asked Gina and Arthur about the sleeping arrangements for the wedding guests who were coming from afar. "As you know; Christine and her father and brothers will stay at the manor," stated Arthur. "I will stay with mom and we will drive down to the manor together." "Jr.'s parents will stay at his place in London," added Gina. "And after the wedding?" asked Mr. Locke. "Christine and I will stay at mom's for two days, then head out to Scotland when her father and brothers leave the manor," mentioned Arthur. "Jr. and I will spend the night in London then take the ferry to Calais and drive to Coudekerque-Branch (where his parents live) and use that as a jumping off place for the 10 days we will be gone," added Gina.

"What were you up to in your office, if you don't mind me asking?" asked Arthur. "Do you remember that small room in the servant's quarters that I said I would get to later?" added Gina. "Well now is later. It's practically empty but certainly smells like it has been closed for years, which it has. I'm not sure what I want to use it for, storage probably, but I'm going to clean it out and let it air for a while. The wallpaper is peeling and there was a squeak or two in the floor; otherwise it seems in good shape. I will need you or dad to make me some shelves, if that's okay?" "No problem," added Mr. Locke and Arthur at the same time. "Just let us know when you're ready." "I'm going to go back up and check out that squeaky floor," stated Gina.

"I've been meaning to ask, how is your painting progressing?" Mrs. Locke asked. "It's coming along," mentioned Gina. "I'm not sure when I will have it finished. I hope to do so before my wedding." "I can't wait to see it," replied Mrs. Lock.

Afterwards Gina brought in a crowbar to pry up any squeaky boards she may find. There was only the one, so she wasn't worried that she might have to have the whole room redone. The floor board came up pretty easily. Gina realized that she should have brought a flashlight up with her. But, after brushing away some cobwebs, a little nervously she started to feel around. It startled her when her hand came in contact with something hard. With a bit of excess strength she managed to pull the item through the opening she made. Blowing the dust off, her curiosity peeked; Gina found that it was a tin box. She tried to open it but found it locked. She didn't want to damage the box and it was getting late, so she set it aside and decided to ask her father to help her open it the next day.

CHAPTER

40

Charlotte, Annabelle and Sharon have established a routine. Sharon loves having a baby around and keeps encouraging Charlotte to go for a walk or to the store for her, so she can have Annabelle to herself. Annabelle at one year old has started to walk. Sharon says she feels younger chasing a one year old around. Philip and Charlotte have insisted that she promise not to over-do it.

Philip has been working for the past two weeks and tells his family that he didn't realize how much he enjoyed landscaping.

Adam and Aaron have also settled into their college routine. It is the first time they have lived away from home and they are really enjoying it. Both boys had become involved in sports and Adam and Trisha have formed the study group they had discussed previously. Aaron told Adam that he has two girls in his class. He didn't realize females would like that type of work. "Of course," stated Adam. "Females like to be able to do any job. They want to be considered equal with males. Kudos to them, I say."

Trisha and Adam liked spending a lot of their time together, but also had separate interests. Adam had joined the rugby team and Trisha joined the writer's club. When they were having lunch in the rotunda, Trisha confessed that she missed her mother. Her mother now has an e-mail address, so they can communicate easily. "My mom seems to be settling into her new job," stated Trisha. "She sounded happy when

89

I talked to her last evening. How are your parents and sister liking England?" "As you know, dad is from England so it's a homecoming for him, but mom is enjoying it. She is getting used to the different food and especially the sayings, like, knackered. She is also finding it hard to get accustomed to the frequent use of "you all right?" When dad first said that mom thought it was a curse word. Grandma had to explain it because dad was laughing too hard to speak. I find that mom is more relaxed than before. I know she misses her mother, but with the internet, it seems like she's really not that far away. Grandma is already planning a trip here for Christmas," added Adam.

41

After dinner one night, Mrs. Locke, Gina and Christine went into the conservatory to relax while the men took the dogs for a walk. The ladies wanted to make sure all was finalized for the wedding which would be in three days' time.

"So what's going to happen over the next two days?" asked Mrs. Locke. "Well, Arthur and Jr. will go to London to return here the morning of the wedding," stated Gina. "Arthur planned to drive down on the morning of our wedding with his mother and Trisha, and Jr. will also be driving down that morning." "I cautioned them both to be sure they give themselves plenty of time to arrive," added Christine. "I am stressed enough as it is, so I do not want anything to go wrong." "I feel the same way," Gina added. "It's natural for brides to get nervous," Mrs. Locke mentioned. "Just try not to worry. You both will look very beautiful and even if there is a small glitch, the wedding will still go on."

"The flowers are going to be delivered late afternoon the day before. We will put them in the cool room," stated Mrs. Locke. "I can make the Cranachan (a traditional Scottish dessert that Christine told me about) a day ahead, as well as another rhubarb/strawberry pie and an apple pie. You never know how hungry people can get." "What about the musicians?" asked Christine. "They'll be here about ninety minutes before the ceremony, and of course will stay for the reception, to play and enjoy some refreshments," stated Mrs. Locke. "Also, the photographer will arrive about the same time."

"Is it true that Dorothy has moved to Calais?" Gina asked her mother. "Yes, she was telling me about it at your engagement dinner. Her pen-pal has a B & B and asked Dorothy to come and help her run it. Since Trisha will be boarding at Maggie's while attending college and her brothers are with their father, Dorothy decided it would be a good time to go. Anyway, Calais is only a short ferry ride away, so Trisha and her brothers can visit quite easily," added Mrs. Locke.

"Doesn't Trisha start classes about a week after your weddings?" Mrs. Locke queried. "Yes," replied Christine. "Arthur told me she and her mother set her room up. Maggie gave her carte blanch to decorate as she chooses; so she would feel at home. Arthur and I are glad that Maggie won't be living alone." "I don't think Trisha would have time to miss her mother what with starting college and I heard she and one of Philip's sons have become quite close. He and his brother will also be attending Croydon," added Mrs. Locke.

"I must check on the room for your family, Christine," mentioned Mrs. Locke. "I understand that they will be arriving quite early." "Let us help," suggested Christine. "No need," replied Mrs. Locke. "It's just a matter of giving the room a quick look over, it won't even take a minute. No, you two go do what you need or just stay for another cuppa, I'll see you in the morning."

42

While putting the finishing touches on the breakfast table, Mrs. Locke heard the excited barking of the dogs. That must be Christine's family, she thought. I'll go out and make sure they come in for breakfast. She walked out to laughing kids and barking dogs. It seemed like a contest between the boys and dogs as to who wants the most attention. Mr. Locke was standing aside with Christine's father taking it all in with big grins on their faces.

"Hi, dad," shouted Christine over the excitement of the dogs and her brothers. "How was the drive?" "It went well, however, but not fast enough for your brothers," stated her father. "They wanted to get here quicker so they could have more time playing with the dogs. You're looking well, my dear," added her father as he gave her a big hug. "I am so happy for you. Your mother would have been proud," he added, wiping away a tear. "Thanks dad," put in Christine. "Where is Arthur?" asked her father. "He's in the dining room with the others waiting for breakfast. Mrs. Locke is holding serving until you arrived, so we best head in there," stated Christine.

After a leisurely breakfast, Jr. and Arthur prepared to head out to London. They will return the morning of their wedding. Jr. gave Gina a final kiss and told her that he would miss her and hoped the time flew by fast. Arthur and Christine were also saying goodbye.

Mr. Locke and Christine's dad went off to do man stuff and her brothers took off with the dogs. Mrs. Locke went upstairs to see to the airing closet, but she actually went up for a short nap. Christine and Gina cleaned up the breakfast dishes and put the kitchen in order. Then they both went to their rooms to finish packing for their honeymoons.

Christine took the protective cover off her wedding dress to gaze at it one more time. She was happy with the A-line dress with a straight skirt she chose. She was also very pleased how the dressmaker was able to incorporate some of her clan colors. They were down into the V and continued down to the waist of the dress and then around the waist. Christine couldn't wait for her father to see it. The skirt of the A-line was of silk. She sat looking at her dress hoping her mother was there to witness her happy day. She allowed herself a short cry, and then she decided to take a luxurious bubble bath before turning in for the night.

Meanwhile, Gina had finished her packing and decided to go up to her studio. She just couldn't forget that box. She had decided not to ask her father for any help. If she couldn't open it now, she would leave it until she came back from her honeymoon. The wedding day will keep her busy enough so she won't have time to think about that box. She then decided to take a long bubble bath after she took one last look at her wedding dress. She felt her choice of a simple sheath dress with antique lace on the bodice and a slim satin skirt was just her style.

CHAPTER

43

Today was the day. She and Christine were finally getting married. When Gina looked out her window, all she saw was cloud and wind. At that moment her mother knocked on her door. Gina confided her worries to her mom, who told her the weather report called for sunshine with no breeze. That helped Gina to relax. Mrs. Locke had a special breakfast set out for Gina and Christine. They stopped at Christine's bedroom on their way downstairs. Gina repeated the information her mother gave her about the weather forecast to Christine. Both girls breathed a huge sigh of relief.

During breakfast Mrs. Locke managed to get the girls to relax by telling them some of the antics Mr. Locke had told her that Christine's brothers had gotten into. Mr. Locke with Christine's father and brothers have taken the dogs out for a longer walk, and then they will enjoy a hearty breakfast of ham and eggs with orange juice and whole wheat toast. After breakfast, Mr. Locke, Christine's father and brothers will set up the chairs out by the gazebo.

"When do you expect the guests to start arriving?" Gina asked her mother. "Sr. and Mrs. Keyes will arrive around noon, so they can rest before the 2 p.m. ceremony. I expect DS Dunes and his wife and son will arrive any time after that. Maggie and Trisha will be coming with

Arthur. Arthur and Jr. will enter through the conservatory and go up to Arthur's room to get ready," answered her mother.

Mrs. Locke came up to Gina's room where she and Christine were in the process of getting ready. A lady that Mrs. Locke knows from Cockernhoe came early giving Mrs. Locke time to help the girls get dressed. The photographer was busy snapping pictures of Mrs. Locke and the two brides. Trisha was sent upstairs to check on the progress of the brides. "They were as ready as can be," said Mrs. Locke. She told Trisha that when they hear the music, the girls will come down the back stairs to meet Mr. Locke and Christine's father in the kitchen; who will then walk them down the aisle. Trisha told them that the grooms both looked nervous.

Both the fathers were stunned at the presence of their beautiful daughters. Mrs. Locke could see the beginning of tears from the fathers and the brides. She left the girls with their fathers and went to join the rest of the guests.

"I hear the music," stated Mr. Locke. "That's our cue. I am honored to be escorting such a beautiful woman down the aisle." "As am I," added Christine's father. "My dear Christine, you look as beautiful as your mother did on our wedding day." "No tears, dad," whispered Christine." I don't want to ruin my makeup." "Let's go," suggested Mr. Locke. "We don't want to keep your grooms to waiting too much longer."

The Pastor had never officiated over a double wedding before, but all in all it went quite smoothly. Double wedding, double happiness.

"Please stand with me and join in welcoming the newly wed couples, Mr. & Mrs. J. Keyes and Mr. & Mrs. A. Graves," announced the pastor.

44

After the married couples drove away, most of the guests followed suit, except Christine's family. They planned to leave in the morning. After Angus and his sons took the dogs for a walk Mrs. Locke decided to do a cleanup. "What are you doing dear?" asked Mr. Locke. "I just want to get a start on the laundry." Mrs. Locke replied. "Just leave it," stated Mr. Locke. "We've had several busy weeks, and I am sure it can wait until tomorrow, come and sit with me." "You're right," answered Mrs. Locke. "I'll make us a pot of tea and bring some of the left over desserts out to the conservatory. I'm sure Angus and the boys will be hungry when they get back from walking the dogs." "That sounds like a plan," murmured Mr. Locke. "Tomorrow you can have at it."

"What plans do you have for today?" Mrs. Locke asked her husband. "After Angus and sons leave, I'm going to take the dogs for a walk and get started with some general cleanup of the yard," he announced. "My plans are to strip the beds and clean the bathrooms," stated Mrs. Locke. "I want everything to be ready for when the newlyweds return."

As Mrs. Locke went to collect the linens from Gina's room, she noticed a box sitting on Gina's nightstand. It looked familiar, so Mrs. Locke picked it up and even before opening it, she knew she had seen this box before. She put it down, continued with her work but decided she would ask Gina about it when she arrives home. All day that box was on her mind. Later, as she and Mr. Locke were discussing the newlyweds, she remembered where she had seen such a box. It was her memento box from when she was 18 years old. It had gone missing after her wedding. They searched and searched, but after a while, decided that it was gone forever. Even after so much time, she didn't need to see the mementoes; she remembered everything that was in the box.

But, it couldn't hurt just to have a peak, could it she thought. Her 18th year was a very special year. It was the year she went to Europe for a 6 month tour with her aunt, and when she returned, that was when she met Mr. Locke. So, to open the box would be like reliving that time of her life. She convinced herself that Gina wouldn't mind if she opened it, since it was hers.

She decided she would sleep on it and after a rather fitful sleep, and after waving goodbye to Angus and sons they retired in the conservatory with a second cup of tea, Margaret told her husband all about the box, her memento box, and asked for his advice. "Well," he asked, "If you still have the key and since it is your box, open it. What do you think?" "I think that's a great idea," replied Margaret. "But I want you with me when I do open it. A lot of the contents I added were after we met and up until a few years after our wedding." "I would love to be there for the opening," stated Morris. "You go get the key and I will meet you in the conservatory."

"I found it," Margaret said, as she entered the conservatory waving the key. "I'm so nervous. Here goes. Wow, this is the ticket stub from our first date. Remember the play you brought me to in London?" "I do remember the trouble we both had to get the same day off," answered Morris. "I also remember that it was raining so hard that we got completely soaked running for the car."

"Do you remember?"

"I remember."